Clint Faraday
book seven
Comedy of Terrors

When does the act stop being funny? After the first
murder ... or later?
Clint goes on a vacation in the mountains of Calderas
with some people who want to visit Panamá.
Some vacation!

Clint Faraday
book seven
Comedy of Terrors
(c)2010 & 2011 by C. D. Moulton

This is a work of fiction. Any resemblances to persons, living or dead, is purely coincidental except where otherwise stated.

Clint Faraday
book seven
Comedy of Terrors

Contents

About the author

CD was born in Lakeland, Florida. His education is in genetics and botany. He has traveled over much of the world, particularly when he was in music as a rock rhythm guitarist with some well-known bands in the late sixties and early seventies. He has worked as a high steel worker and as a longshoreman, clerk, orchidist, bar owner, salvage yard manager and landscaper – among other things.

CD began writing fiction in 1984 and has more than 115 books published as of this time in SciFi, murder, orchid culture and various other fields.

He now resides in Bocas del Toro and David, Panamá, where he continues research into epiphytic plants. He loves the culture of the indigenous people and counts a majority of his closer friends among that group. Several have "adopted" him as their father. He funds those he can afford through the universities where they have all excelled. "The Indios are very intelligent people, they are simply too poor (in material things and money. Culturally, they are very wealthy) to pursue higher education."

CD loves Panamá and the people. He plans to spend the rest of his life in the paradise that is Panamá

- Estrelita Suarez V.

CD is involved in research of natural cancer cure at this time. It has proven effective in all cases, so far. It is based on a plant that has been in use for thousands of years, is safe, available, and cheap. He has studied botany, and was cured of a serious lymphoma with use of the plant, *Ambrosia peruviana*.

Information about this cure is free on the FaceBook page, Ambrosia peruviana for cancer. CD asks only that all who try it please report on its effectiveness on that group.

Comedy of Terrors

A Beautiful Morning

Clint Faraday, retired detective from Florida, lazed on his deck with his first coffee of the day to watch the not-so-colorful sunrise, today. The breeze off the Caribbean was warm, so there was no rain approaching before noon. This time of the year, rain came from the Caribbean. It would be a beautiful day.

Judi Lum, his attractive neighbor, came to call from her deck a hundred meters farther along the bay, "Good morning!" and to shake a finger at him for being on his deck, as on most mornings, nude.

Why bother to dress until you know what to dress for? He was in his own house and would wear as much or as little as he chose. He wasn't built any different than any other guy. He didn't have anything to hide.

He waved and called that he thought he would go out past Tierra Oscura for the day. Did she want to go along? It would be all day.

"I've got company," she called back. "They'll want to see the country, the real Panamá, not Bocas. Today will be here. They get in on the eleven o'clock flight. We can meet for dinner at, say, seven thirty, at The Rip Tide, Okay? We can decide what they want to do tomorrow, or whatever. They're very nice people. You'll even like their teenage kids. I think they're as balanced and mature as any I've ever met that age."

Clint agreed, lazed around another half hour, read his e-mail and answered a couple, then took his boat down past Tierra Oscura to visit friends on the islands there, awhile, went to Chiriqui Grande for a couple of hours at lunchtime, then came slowly back to Bocas Town at five o'clock. He cleaned the boat, cleaned up, himself, a bit, and checked his calls.

Nothing important.

Next was his e-mail. Mostly spam. One from his oddball friend, Dave, saying that he'd heard something sort of strange and didn't know what to make of it, so would pass it on, seeing Judi was somehow involved. He knew how Clint protected her – even though she didn't need any protection. She was thoroughly capable of taking care of herself.

Some people he didn't know had been looking for Clint, who wasn't around. He was asked to tell him, "Those Campbell people Judi met at the airport are not here to look at the country. They came here to hide from some dangerous people. They are not who they're supposed to be." That was it.

Clint sent back that he'd check into it, if it seemed particularly advisable. How could he identify who sent the message? A description or something would do, seeing Dave said he didn't know them.

He put on some fresh shorts and a shirt and went to The Rip Tide to meet the Campbells, who were a close family who seemed regular enough people, to Clint. He was about forty, and took care of himself, she was about two years younger, and was also in great shape, as were her daughter and two sons. They weren't really vegans, but were interested in seafoods. They didn't eat red meat or certain vegetables.

Mark, the eldest son (19), said they had learned some things in Jamaica about certain types of plants in the diet. They could wreak havoc with the digestive system, in certain combinations. The mother, Ann, said to not make it sound like they were fanatics. The daughter Cori

(16), said it was in Haiti that they ran across the fanatics. Matt, the father, said they ran across nutcases most places, but tried to use logic in such things. If you were told oranges were really bad for the teeth, check it out. He was raised in an orange grove, where he ate several a day for years. He had perfect teeth. The net information said it was bad, but depended, as a lot of those things did, on genetics. Mike, the younger son (15), said a lot of that crap was crap, anyhow. If you don't like squash, don't eat it. Don't make up some kind of horror story as an excuse. Different people liked different things. He didn't like breadfruit, until he tried some of the fried stuff that afternoon. It was delicious. All he'd tried before tasted like library paste, to him. It was a big joke, anyhow. The human race had been eating all of it for millennia, and were still around – if you used a loose enough definition of "human." Some of the people they'd met recently would play hell trying to fit his definition.

They had a couple from the islands with them, who weren't there for dinner, though Judi had met them and invited them. She said they were a little strange, but that may be because they'd never been off the island. In other words, the Campbells were normal, if a bit health-conscious, people. Clint tended to like them. They had great sense of humor. That always appealed to him.

They wanted to go into the mountains, where Judi told them Clint knew almost every Indio in the two close provinces. They wanted to see the real Panamá and meet the real Panamanians. They decided to start in the morning. They would take a bus to Gualaca, then would find a ride on toward Calderas. He hadn't been there in almost two years. He wanted to see how some of his friends were doing. The scenery was unbelievable, from the tops of some of the mountains. At Obilio's place, they could see both the Caribbean and the Pacific, if there weren't too many clouds lower than the top of the mountain. He warned them that it was a long walk through native cloud and rain forests, where there was usually not enough of a path to follow. They could ride horses, but that would cost quite a bit. He would ask Pablo and Maria Garza (the couple traveling with them. They were darker Caribbean island people, about twenty two or so) if they wanted to come. Matt said they had enough to hire horses.

Clint said that Luis would go along with them. He had the horses and liked to explore, along with Clint. He was Indio, but Clint was always seeing things that he wouldn't notice. He learned a lot, that way. He was a happy-go-lucky type, with a great sense of humor.

The night was very pleasant. Clint told them what to take. They'd take his boat to Chiriqui Grande, then ride the bus to Gualaca. Remember that they would have to carry what they took in a climb that would take at least four hours. Lugging a load of stuff that you wouldn't use could take the fun out of any trip. They would leave from the ferry dock at six thirty in the morning. That would time it right for the rest of the day.

Clint pulled into the dock at six twenty five, with Judi aboard. She'd decided that, seeing she'd never been to that particular place, she'd like to come along. Clint met Pablo and Maria Garza, from the Dominican Republic. They were small, attractive people, who were very nervous, for some reason. They tended to be very quiet. They seemed a bit reserved and ... wary, for some reason. Maria dropped her small maleta and crossed herself before she picked it up.

There were very few on the dock, that early. A couple

of men were sitting on the end. One man and a teenage boy were throwing hand lines for fish. A man and woman were walking past, toward downtown. Clint had a talent for seeing everything about a place. It had been a handy talent to have, in some of his cases.

Everyone in their party were in the boat. They were pulling out into the bay. Mike said, "The adventure begins! I think I like this place more than any of the places we ever went – and we've gone to a lot of places!"

"A four hour climb, riding horses, to a mountaintop, where you can see the Caribbean and Pacific by just turning around? I think it'll be fantastic!" Mark agreed.

"I like this kind of thing," Cori agreed. "I get awfully sick of just hanging around a hotel."

"There won't be phones and boomboxes out there," Ann warned.

"Thank god! We can get away from salsa and regatón for awhile!"

"We will be to Obilio's by three thirty," Luis decided. "I will call him to say we are coming, so Lila can have the rooms ready. He has two and the bodega, so the men will sleep in his room and the women in the other and the ones who can't decide which they are can sleep with whoever. Whoever wants to can sleep in the bodega. (Clint almost let a grin escape at the subtle joke.) I will return the horses to Manuel's finca, almost three quarters of the way there, and will return with the horses when you wish to go. Clint knows how to put the flag to tell me to come and how many horses will be needed..

"Obilio was saying a few days ago that he would like to see Clint again. He will be very pleased that you are coming."

"You have phone service out here?" Matt asked.

"Only on the top. If he's in the house, he will receive. If not, we will not be able to tell him that we have already decided on all the arrangements." (Clint was the only one who got the joke – except maybe Judi. She had an amused look on her face.)

"I have a lot of food. We'd better be able to pack the horses where it won't be in the way and won't get tangled in the shrubs," Judi suggested. "I know, from the pictures Clint showed me from his last trip here, that it gets very close, in places."

"I am bringing another horse to carry a lot of things," Luis said. "You have enough food for the Policia National here! Will you be staying for the year?"

They all laughed, then Mike looked confused for a few seconds and let a small additional laugh escape. "Ann insisted," Judi said. "I've met Obilio, but none of the

Campbells have. t's proper that they bring food, in the states."

It would be slightly insulting for a friend who was only very occasionally there to bring food. This would make it an acceptable and even a thoughtful thing for them to bring extra food. Strangers, new people who were friends of friends, or people who came, often brought food. Occasional close friends did not.

Judi had insisted on practicality. No steaks or spoilables that couldn't be kept for three days.

"The food is fresh and in good state," Luis said, with perfect innocence. Mike slapped him on the back and laughed, which made the rest catch the joke. That brought the problem that Obilio grew yuca, yampi, most fruits, coffee and most of what they ate, right there. Rice, onions, potatoes, pasta, flour, dried beans of types that Obilio wouldn't grow (Those that grew at altitude, he had in excess. He traded some things with neighbors, who lived lower) and such. Ann had insisted that they take four times as much as Judi suggested. She said Obilio's wife would surely know people who would use it, if it was too much for them. Cori said that crowd could out-eat the policia, any day.

Hard to argue. Clint was impressed that these people, who he was warned were not what they seemed, were actually very considerate people.

A man brought another horse to leave with Luis, who began to place the extra food and bags on it. Judi and Ann were talking with a few of the native women, Mike, Cori and Mark checked over the saddles and gear, Clint and Matt helped pack the riding horses. Pablo and Maria were standing to one side. They were mostly very quiet. They seemed to be studying the passersby. Some of the Indio women were in colorful traditional garb. There were few strangers around the almacen, this far from so-called "civilization."

They soon were ready. They headed along the road for half a kilometer, then took a path to the side, through a log gate, and started up the mountain. They would go around this one partway up, then cross a high valley to the mountain Obilio occupied. Other than their party, there were only Indios here for kilometers in any direction. The scenery was magnificent and humbling. It was quiet, except for a few birds and insects. They even talked quietly. At times, when Luis heard someone working across the valley he would call the "Oye!" the people here used to greet each other from a distance. He was always answered. Cori wanted to learn how to call the greeting, but Luis explained that the women didn't use that call. He managed to ride close to Cori, when he could. They exchanged a lot of jokes. All of the Campbells spoke excellent Spanish. Cori was learning some of the Indio dialect from Luis. At one point, Clint got Matt aside and asked if Cori knew how to handle a proposition. She was goodlooking, and 16 was past the legal age, in the comarcas. Matt assured him there would be no problem. No offense would be taken. Cori could handle things, very well. She wasn't raised like most gringas. She was as independent as anyone you would meet.

Luis was in his early twenties. Clint was perfectly well aware that he would come on to Cori. Matt told Ann about it. She laughed. Cori could handle herself. Luis was a very handsome man. Too bad he didn't come on to her!

Matt laughed, and said the Indian women were very sexy. That long thick black hair was one hell of a turn-on. They joked a bit about it. Mark came over and was told about the joke. He said Cori probably was no virgin, but the family was on the "Don't ask, don't tell" bus. They all knew how important protection was and what kind of situations not to allow to develop. It was an individual decision as to what and with whom you decided to do. Mike, who was the most talkative of the family, talked to Clint a lot of the way. He explained that their father always taught them that the fact they were so fortunate meant they owed others some thought. The result was that they went all over the Americas and made friends, for the most part. Others they had met traveling were exactly what so many people thought gringos were. Overbearing, arrogant and totally selfish. He really liked people like Luis, who could make little jokes about anything. People with good senses of humor were generally good people to be around. Cori had some experience. She might even take Luis up on it. It was her decision.

Clint said he'd met enough of the asshole type. There were places where gringos congregated, communities, and a lot of them were exactly like that. Pains in the ass. Mike said it right. "And all gringos have to live with what those few are."

Pablo was riding silently beside them, where the trail was wide enough. He said some gringos were worse than the curses from the brujas. He should know! Many of the ones who came to the Dominican Republic thought all natives were slaves to be ordered around. They were very deeply resented. Then the Campbells came and showed them all gringos were not alike.

They passed two younger Indios (early twenties) going down the mountain. They stopped to chat. One of them was wearing a wig and makeup. He was introduced as Rigo, better known as Lola. He was going to David for a transvestite show at the Texas. Clint didn't know how the Campbells would take that, but they seemed merely slightly interested. Ann even showed Rigo how to use eyeliner and shade in a way that made him attractive without making him look like a cheap whore.

He said that was the object. Look like a cheap whore or a movie star.

"But who you attract as an attractive girl is not the same as when you look like a puta," she pointed out. "Of course, I don't know if you want to attract a certain type."

"I'd like to attract someone who looks like either of those!" he replied, pointing to Mike and Mark.

Mike grinned. He said, "Yo, Mom! I think I don't care for all this mountain stuff. Maybe I could go to David with these guys!"

"When you're eighteen. You can't go as a minor. You have to wait until they get back and you can stay at their house here. Use protection. I've warned you about AIDS and herpes." She giggled and smirked.

"Then I don't think I'll go to David!" Rigo cried.

Pablo and Maria (who seldom said a word, anyway) were the only ones who seemed uneasy or in any way bothered by them. They moved away and waited, looking at some of the many bromeliads and orchids in the trees by the trail.

They joked a bit more, then went onward and upward. Mike said he had gay friends. That they were just people. Who anyone slept with was their own personal business – which is the Indio philosophy.

"It is not natural," Pablo said. "They are cursed!"

"Oh, bullshit," Mike said. "They aren't any different than anyone else. You'll get all preachy about what's natural, then brag about screwing some whore in the ass or getting a blow job.

"Got news for you! That isn't anymore natural than the gay people are."

"Rigo is a handsome kid. That's the sad thing. He won't have kids to pass it along," Mark said.

"Oh, he'll probably do the drag queen thing for a year or two, then get married – as much as they do – and have a couple of kids," Judi said. "They seem to do that. The Indios like sex. They don't pretend otherwise. We're the ones with the taboos and inhibitions."

"He's so openly gay, yet a girl will marry him?" Matt asked. Pablo snorted.

"They think nothing of it. It's sort of a stage that some of them go through. they recognize six sexes. They're genetically bisexual, to one degree or another," Clint said. "They don't think it's even a little unusual. Some people like yuca, some don't. Some people like fish, some don't. That's what life is like."

"Oh?" Mike asked, innocently. "Do you sleep with many of them? Often?"

"Only when I'm in the higher mountains and in their culture," Clint replied, leaving them all uncertain of how to react, so they changed the subject. They didn't know if he was putting them on or serious. Pablo seemed actually shocked. He dropped back a bit. Matt asked if it was natural to make everything center around sex out there. He had seen that in several places.

Clint had slept with a few of them, but sleep was all they did. They slept wrapped up in each other, in the mountains. It got cold at night, and they usually didn't have but one blanket to share. If something developed from that closeness, it happened. Clint had wondered what was going to happen, at times. He agreed that it was pleasant to sleep close to someone.

So far as talking about sex a lot, what else was there to do for recreation in these mountains? They were sexy people, so they talked and joked about sex. It was a thing they were comfortable with. Almost everyone thought of sex a lot. Why not talk about it? Gringos bragged and lied about it, Indios simply made it part of their conversations and jokes. They didn't have a need to try to impress anyone with the fact they were no different than other people – except for the honesty part.

They stopped, several times, to take pictures or to just enjoy the view. They passed across a valley from a waterfall that dropped more than a hundred meters. The sun was at just the right angle to have a very bright rainbow at the bottom. Judi stopped several times to take pictures of various plants. Orchids worth thousands in the states were as much as weeds here.

They finally reached the house. It was down in the trees about a hundred meters from the top. The convection winds would make being on the top extremely uncomfortable, at times. Obilio ran out to embrace Clint and welcome him. He embraced Judi and shook hands with all the Campbells and the Garzas. Ann said she brought some food, because that's what you did in the states. Where to put it? Lila came out to embrace Clint and to meet the others.

Obilio is in his seventies. He thinks nothing of walking four hours up the mountain to his house. The Campbells, on horses, were as much as exhausted. Pablo seemed a little tired. Maria didn't seem affected, one way or another.

Lila showed them the men's room and the women's room and pointed to the creek a little down the mountain. The Indios are clean to almost an extreme. The water is ice cold, but they bathe at least once a day.

Obilio had a small outhouse built over the ravine the creek fell into.

Lila served a drink she made from corn that was delicious and refreshing. They all knew about the chicha, how it was corn, fermented very slightly in water and sugar, then milk was added. Ann was allergic to it, but the rest would like a glass. Ann preferred water, anyhow.

Lila, Judi, Cori and Ann hit it off quickly. They became pals. Cori, unlike a lot of gringas her age, pitched right in around the house. That impressed Lila and Obilio. The few gringas and Latinas her age they knew were little princesses who would be insulted if anyone expected them to do anything.

Clint rested with the others for an hour or so, then said he was going to the top to see the view. Obilio said they could see the Caribbean, this time of the year, but it wasn't very often you could see the Pacific. It was the rainy season that side of the mountains.

There was one small patch in the clouds where the Pacific could be glimpsed. The Caribbean was visible, most of the time. Everyone was thrilled, but went back to the house. Matt was a bit winded, as was Ann. Clint told them they were at an altitude where the air was getting a bit thin. Mike said he felt that and Mark said the only places that had affected him much were at Machu Pichu and La Paz.

They went back for dinner. Pork aguisada, with rice and beans. There was a stew of a number of vegetables that were found in the mountains. Lila had boiled a pan of mustard greens. She knew how Clint liked them. The Indios seldom ate mustard, but it was a weed around the place. She put some pork skin in the pot when she boiled them (at Cori's suggestion) and Judi brought vinegar. Obilio and Lila tasted them that way. They said they would probably be eating them all along, if they'd known how to fix them. The vinegar and pork skin made them very tasty. Cori said mustard greens were called the perfect green. It had everything a green leafy vegetable could have, in the way of healthy vitamins and minerals.

When they went to bed, the men went in one room and the women in the other. Pablo and Maria wanted to stay in the bodega. They weren't used to sleeping in the same room as others since they were very young and slept in the same room as their brothers and sisters. If anyone had a curse on them, the others in the room might suffer when it came.

Judi shook her head. When they went out to the bodega, Mike said that was the kind of thing he heard everywhere on the islands. Some curse or a zombie or a demon was chasing everyone, for one reason or another. People were downright paranoid about it. It was tiresome. They had to live with a lot of terrors – all in their own heads. You could see what it did to the psychology of the people. Everyone on this jaunt was having fun, except them.

Clint was amused when there were only two pallets and two blankets. They had bathed in the stream. Obilio and Clint were on one pallet and Mike joined them. Mark and Matt took the other. Mike said, if anything happened, he wouldn't want it to be with his father or brother. Matt said that was true. Anyone he screwed ended up thinking they were in love with him. That wouldn't be right with a little brother.

When they first got in bed, Clint and Obilio laid close together. Mike grinned and hugged them both. Matt and Mark were a bit apart when they went to bed. They were together, later, after the temperature had dropped into the mid-fifties, when they awoke to a scream from the direction of the bodega sometime after midnight. They all jumped up and ran for the shed.

The moonlight makes things fairly visible, at that altitude. The door to the bodega was open. Pablo was inside, ripped from his neck to his crotch with what looked like three large deep claw tears. His throat was ripped open. He was, too obviously, dead. Maria was nowhere to be seen.

"What the hell did that?!" Mike exclaimed. Judi, Ann, Cori, and Lila came running from the house. Clint stopped them and said Pablo was dead. Go inside and stay there.

"What kind of animal up here could do that?" Mark asked.

"There are no animals up here that could do that," Obilio said. "There is a story of a demon that kills people who invade the natural places. It only kills on dark nights. This is not a dark night. It kills by breaking the neck, not with claws."

"We have to find Maria," Matt said. "There's something I've heard. There's something they were running from. Pablo said he was trying to break a curse on him, a couple of times. A vengeful ghost was chasing him.

"No ghost did that!"

Clint used his cell phone to call the police, who said it was in the comarca. It would be handled by the council. If the council requested, they would come, immediately. Obilio took the phone and identified himself as a member of the council. He asked them to come to investigate this one thing. Clint would represent authority of the council in the matter. They would fly in on a helicopter at dawn. They couldn't land at night on those mountains.

Clint asked if Obilio really had that authority.

"Oh, certainly. I am what you would call the first vice president in your corporations. I am in full charge on this mountain and the parts in the comarca around for most of the close mountains. Javier handles half and I handle half, but he is in charge."

You live and learn! Clint had known Obilio for more than three years. He hadn't known he was second in charge in the comarca!

He called for Judi to bring his camera, took pictures of the scene from all angles, then asked Obilio if he could find some kind of trail where Maria had been taken. Obilio went outside and a short distance away from the bodega and circled around. He had a flashlight Ann brought to him, but said they would have to wait for light. A trail would be nearly impossible to find or follow with no more than the flashlight. The flashlight didn't have the right kind of light to see, like the sunlight did. Mike said the sun had the full spectrum was why plants grew in sunlight and not in artificial light not designed for plants.

"I believe her body would be here, if they wanted to

kill her," he said. Clint thought about it, and nodded.

They went inside to have some very strong coffee and to wait for dawn. Clint asked how they charged their phones up there. Obilio showed him the solar panel with an adapter. It was the kind of panel used to trickle-charge car batteries.

Mike came to sit with them. He was still a little sick from seeing that mutilated body. Obilio sat close. That was the Indio way. They offered comfort by touching. There's no word for "Thank you" in their language. They don't have to say something so obvious. They say such things through contact, even if it is only a slight squeeze of the hand. Clint found many parts of the culture very natural to him. Apparently, Mike did, too.

Dawn was just breaking when they heard the chopper coming across the valley. It would be dark in the bottom of the valley for some time yet, but the mountaintop had the sun, first. The police officer, Samuel Lopez, directed the one detective with them and took pictures, much as Clint had, then searched through the effects of the Garza's. There wasn't much, but the passports had good pictures they could use to try to find Maria. They would take the body back to David. Clint, Mark, and Obilio started the search for a trail to find Maria, as soon as the light was enough. They found two trails. The attacker(s) had come from the direction of the carretera, and left toward Volcan Barú. They could find the trail lower, but there was a stretch where it would be almost impossible to track.

Mark called from a short distance away. He found a small bit of plastic on a bush. There was no plastic up there. It would have to have been put there.

Obilio said the winds would sometimes bring a plastic bag or such, but this was placed with too much force for that. It was a small scrap of pale blue that would not stick to anything in the wind. It was only there for a few hours. The sap was still wet where a leaf was torn off. Clint had to search very carefully to find wet sap that Obilio saw, automatically. It looked like dew from the clouds that sat there until nearly daylight and was, only now, completely drying, to Clint. Obilio said sap contains sugar. Ants eat the sugar. There were two small ants on the twig. Also, light was a very little bit different on sap than on water. Clint couldn't see any difference, but knew Obilio could, whether from a learned more sensitive reception of color or because of genetically different receptors in the eye.

Matt called Mike and said he was to protect the women with his own life, if it came to that. He and Cori would take the .38 and would shoot first and ask questions later, if Lila said someone was not a familiar and trusted face. Cori said she would put up the flag for Luis to come. She was sure they could trust him. Clint agreed.

Clint, Obilio, and Matt followed the trail for two kilometers, until it was hopelessly lost in a small shallow rocky creek. There were a couple more small scraps of plastic to be found before the creek.

"This quebrada reaches another more than a kilometer down the valley, then that one goes to a larger one that goes to the big river," Obilio explained. "If someone was forcing the woman to go, they will not yet be to the river. She has left several scraps of plastic from a bolsa for us to find. Perhaps we can reach the river before they do. There is a very easy path, close. There will be very few scraps. She is trying to have whoever she is with not know she is leaving them. Very small bits can be torn from a bolsa on the carry loops that will not be noticed, where larger pieces will be seen. She is very intelligent. She may be too ... we must be careful. She knows she has to be careful. This is not a good situation for any."

"Now I'm confused," Clint said. "If they knew the area, they would know of the faster path. If not, they wouldn't even know about this route out of here. It doesn't compute, somehow."

"Ah!" Obilio exclaimed. "So they are going somewhere before the river that is also very close to the quebrada."

"Are there any houses along here?" Clint asked. Obilio shook his head.

"We passed a cave back a ways. Are there caves?" Matt asked. Obilio said there were a few. Small, but easy to reach from the trail.

"Then it's someone from here, and they're in a cave. I've been here four times and didn't know about them," Clint said. "We can go spelunking." He checked his Glock. Matt grinned and took a .32 automatic from his belt in back. Clint had noticed it when they left Obilio's, but had waited to see if he would let them know he had it. Clint was relieved that he did. Obilio simply nodded and went to the little cliff ledge to study the valley below. He waved for them to come, then went down an almost invisible trail into the forest. He said they could reach the more likely of the caves very quickly from where they were. It was mostly downhill. The mountain here was not so steep it would be difficult to stay on the path.

"Very quickly" turned out to be almost an hour. There was evidence that someone had been there, recently, but no Maria. Matt went slowly around and found a very small plastic bit on a branch. "Does this mean they came from that way or that they left that way?"

Obilio searched back along the path and finally said, "Both." They followed the path, several times losing it and having to circle to find it again.

They spent most of the day, searching. They didn't find anything else. Late in the afternoon, they came to a small group of huts with a path that led to a trail that led to the carretera. Obilio said that was where the bruja (witch woman) lived.

"Oh, shit!" Matt exclaimed. "He was always worried about a curse, he's dead, Maria's missing – and the trail leads to a witch! This is a little beyond weird!"

"His curse was from the Dominican Republic," Clint pointed out.

"But he was scared here. He said the curse followed him anywhere." from Matt. "He was scared in Jamaica and in Guatemala. He was as much as terrified, but he seemed to believe it was directed more at Maria. She was always a bit fatalistic about it. She said it had to be lifted by the one who placed it and could not be escaped. They're terrified of their voodoo kings and queens on the islands. Haiti is the center."

"Brujas communicate over the whole world," Obilio stated, positively. "I will ask to meet with her, tomorrow. Perhaps she will tell me ... things. Perhaps not."

They went to the trail and back to Obilio's place. Luis was waiting there with Mike and the women. He had four horses.

"I think there was someone over there on that mountain, watching us," Judi said, pointing across the valley to the near mountain that was only two or three hundred meters lower than Obilio's. "Twice, I saw a flash like the sun reflecting off a mirror. Maybe a lens."

Clint nodded. Mike got him aside and said he didn't want to scare the others, but he'd seen someone on the other side of the stream, where they bathed. He said it wasn't an Indio. He was much lighter in color, but he couldn't see much else. He was wearing camouflage clothes that looked too much like military issue. It could be someone from the police. He didn't know if they would leave someone to watch, but didn't think that chopper could carry three. They had to carry Pablo's body on the runners – which meant someone might have ridden in on a runner.

"No one was left on the comarca," Clint replied. "Obilio would have to approve and would know about it."

Mike looked grim, and nodded. Clint was impressed that someone his age was so much in control and so aware of reality. This was no exciting adventure to him. He wasn't lost in some TV show mentality.

Cori got Clint aside a bit later and said almost the same thing. She didn't want to worry anyone. Things were tense enough, without that. She had told Luis, who went casually down to the stream to see if he could find anything.

Ann and Lila also got him alone to tell him the same thing. All of them had noticed something and had acted in a way not to scare all the others. It would be funny as hell, if it weren't so serious.

There wasn't much to be done, with it getting dark. They sat around to talk until they went to bed. Clint and Obilio knew how to find the glow of a fire that was screened toward the house. Both noted the spot across the valley. Judi had seen the reflection off a lens to binoculars, almost certainly.

Obilio said he knew how to get to that little ledge from in back. They would leave before light from the back of the house, so they wouldn't be seen. Matt would have the women moving around the place to be seen, and would dress so that he would look like Clint. at times. Mike wanted to go with them. Obilio said he could go if he knew how to be quiet and how to move where he wouldn't be seen. He said he would surprise them all with what he knew. Mark would go with Lila to talk with the bruja. They would be seen a bit after daylight. in plain sight of the watch ledge. moving along the path toward the place. Judi had Clint's .22 pistol, and was an expert shot. She would know how to protect from certain types of attack. She also knew a few tricks. She would surprise hell out of any attacker who thought she was the helpless woman type.

Clint and Obilio left before dawn, climbing out of a rear window that couldn't be seen from anywhere in the area. They were soon on a covered path through the forest toward the side and behind the ledge. Luis stepped from the forest ahead of them, two hundred meters from the house. Clint had as much as forgotten he was there. He had watched the entire night.

"Someone came to the loma there (pointing at the little hill) perhaps an hour after midnight," he reported. "He did not come closer. He stopped for a moment, then returned. I think he wanted to see if there were any lights in the house or bodega. He was very large."

Obilio told him it was a good thing to know. He could go to the house and sleep a few hours.

Clint and Obilio went on. An hour later, Obilio held up a hand. Clint stopped. They were moving silently along. Most likely, Obilio would have heard or seen something.

Mike made a snapping sign with his hands, as though he were snapping a twig. Obilio nodded and pointed ahead and slightly to the left.

Mike slipped into the forest on that side. Clint moved to stop him, but was too late. Obilio looked surprised, then shrugged. He and Clint waited. A monkey made a "woo-woo" sound ahead and Obilio again looked surprised and waved for Clint to come along.

"Perhaps to the right?" Obilio suddenly said in a hissing whisper, surprising Clint, this time. He was waving to stop.

There was a "Thunk!" sound ahead, then Mike stepped out about a hundred feet ahead and waved for them to come on.

A big black man was unconscious behind a large boulder. Mike had come up behind him, couldn't get close enough, moved away a bit and climbed a tree to make the monkey call, then had come back down to come up behind the watcher when Obilio had drawn him down to behind the boulder. He'd smacked him with a good-sized rock. He would have a concussion, at best.

Mike took a roll of duct tape from his carry sack and taped the man's hand and feet together, then taped his mouth. It was a very professional type of tying.

They went on. Mike was surprising Clint and Obilio with his knowledge and cool attitude. Clint wouldn't have expected that from his reaction to seeing Pablo's mutilated body.

They were still moving silently. Clint couldn't ask questions.

They went into a high valley and across the quebrada to ascend the next mountain. Obilio soon had them moving to the left. He motioned for them to stop. He drew a short line in the dirt, pointed to a large boulder, and put a pebble next to the line, then drew the line around it and motioned downward. He pointed to Mike and the line. He then drew a line with a hook that came to the same spot Mike would be and pointed to Clint. He pointed directly left to a slight animal path. He pointed past the turn Mike would take and to himself, nodded sharply and erased the diagram in the dirt.

Clint moved to the path, Mike went to the boulder path and Obilio went ahead.

Half an hour later, Clint was to the left of the ledge, where there was a frond lean-to with a small fire with a coffee pot on the rocks beside it that couldn't be seen from the house across the valley. Mike waved a white handkerchief one short wave from just above.

There was no sign, otherwise, so they waited. Ten minutes later, Obilio strolled from the far side toward the lean-to. Two men stepped out and asked him what he wanted. They were both blacks and both pretty big.

"This is comarca land and you are here. I am council. I ask what YOU are doing here, not the other way around!"

"It's none of your business!" one of them snapped. He took a knife from his belt and started to advance toward Obilio.

There was a shot. He dropped. Mike yelled, "No movir! Movir y morir!" (Don't move! Move and die!) The other one stood perfectly still. Obilio picked up the knife the other had and advanced toward the still standing man. Mike and Clint came from their places and watched.

"I will ask the questions. You will answer," Obilio announced. "Who are you and what are you doing here?"

The man shook his head and said nothing. Obilio flipped the knife and there was a cut along the side of the hood's neck that was oozing blood.

"Who are you and what are you doing here?" he asked

again.

The hood started to say something, then shook his head again.

There was another flick of the knife. There was a cut along the side of the hoods face that was a bit deeper and was oozing more blood.

"Who are you and what are you doing here?" Obilio asked, calmly.

The hood sobbed and said he was Armand Montaigne. He was watching the house across the valley for another person. The dead man was Liam Costigne. He was just watching. They didn't know what it was about. The papaloi ordered them to come and to watch. He was in Haiti. They would be turned into zombies if they didn't do as he ordered.

"Who is the one back along the trail!"

"Aurelio Smith, from Colón. He is to show is how to move here. There is also Antoin. Antoin is black."

This was asked in Spanish and answered in bastard English, much like wadi-wadi.

"Get your slimy ass out of Panamá. You can tell the police about your buddy here, if you like. If not, the people here will bury him and nothing will be known, except he came into the mountains and was never heard of again," Clint said. "Is the bruja involved?

"The most important thing you can answer is where is Maria Garza and is she alright?"

"She is the woman they are after? I don't know anything, except she has to answer questions from ... some people in Haiti. I know nothing of any bruja. Perhaps Aurelio spoke with her."

Clint nodded. He warned the hood to get out of Panamá, again. Today.

Mike, Obilio, and Clint turned away and went back

along the path, without another word. Clint wanted to ask a lot of other questions of Armand Montaigne, but realized it would be a bad idea. It would also be more likely Aurelio Smith could answer them faster and better.

But Aurelio Smith was gone.

"Damn! I wanted to ask dear Aurelio a thing or two!" Clint said.

"Antoin. Aurelio probably isn't black," Mike said.

"She knows something, but will say nothing, other than that she sensed a little spell on someone. It was not a dangerous spell, in itself. It was a way that the person could be located from anywhere, or something," Lila reported, about her interview with the bruja. "She is afraid, I think. That is a bad sign.

"A very big black man went to her with another who was part black, but not so large. Verna said that the smaller one spoke in a strange language that was much like Ingles. The black man spoke very good Spanish."

Clint thanked her. That would be Aurelio Smith and Antoin. Antoin would be a bit bigger than Aurelio. Every little bit added to what they had to know.

Luis had gone to his finca. He would return before dark. It was late enough that he would be there in a few minutes, probably, though he could travel easily enough with the moonlight. It was clear, this high on the mountain. Cori was cooking a meal for them. Judi and Matt had been almost going crazy, worrying about them. Judi heard a shot and was afraid it wasn't from any of their guns. Ann was helping a woman who had been hurt when she had fallen over a vine across the path, below, partway between Luis's place and Obilio's.

Clint asked about the vine. It was just a vine that had fallen when the limb it was on fell. The woman was carrying laundry to the stream and hadn't seen it.

Clint remembered the witch had two visitors, one not among those they'd seen. He would be the one with Maria. He would be the one who got Antoin out. He would be the one who put a vine warning trap across their path. He would be the one with answers. He would be close.

In the morning, they would find who that man was, and what he knew. Somehow. This was the comarca . Obilio could get the people here to cooperate. They had very little fear of the witch woman. She was more a medicine woman who knew a few things about what was considered to be magic here.

They had to make a plan, of sorts. This was a long way from over. None of them knew what was going on, in reality.

"I want all the women to go back to David in the morning. They can stay there among lots of other people. Don't anyone go anywhere alone," Clint suggested. "We have to find what's behind it. We're flying blind, at this point. Murder is part of it, already, so don't get to feeling safe. You're not."

"What makes you think that?" Mark asked.

"They would have taken Maria and would be gone by now. They wouldn't be watching this house and us," Judi answered. "They think all of us, or one of us, or any combination knows something."

"Somebody does," Clint agreed. "The problem is that the person or persons with information don't know what it is. We can spend awhile trying to figure what it could be.

"For instance, we know it has something to do with Maria and very probably Pablo. If they're hanging around because of that, they'll go to David when you do. If they stay, they think I know something. I think only this character who went to the bruja is still here. He would have gotten Antoin away. We know he's in it. He'll probably know what it's about. The others didn't."

It would have to wait for morning. Clint asked a few questions, but didn't learn much. The phone was working well enough that he could call out. He asked the police to check on the ones whose names he knew. They had already checked them, to an extent. They were aliens who didn't go to places tourists went, after they stated they were tourists, at entry into Panamá.

Clint said they came as a group. He must have information about the smaller black. There was reason to believe that he may be the one who abducted Maria Garza. Five minutes later, he knew the man was Quentin LeMonde, from Haiti, but had a passport that said he was Denis Jaques, from Jamaica, also. Both seemed to be legitimate passports. It was under investigation, but could be used as a means to detain him, if and when that seemed advisable. There was an Aurelio Smith and an Antoin Fontaine. Antoin was a very large black man. Aurelio is not so large and is part black. Moreno.

Samuel had called Sergio, in Bocas, and was advised that Clint was quite often used as an investigator by the Policia Nationál (a slight exaggeration. He had only worked with the local police at Bocas Town – who were Policia Nationál! It was true!) to great advantage. Samuel would cooperate, to the extent it was legal.

Okay. He knew the name(s) of the person who went to the bruja.

"Ever hear of a Denis Jaques in Jamaica?" Clint asked the group. Cori said she might have met him. If he was a slender man who spoke wadi-wadi all the time. He had said something to Pablo at the fish market. Pablo said his name was Quent or something such, so it was probably somebody else.

Clint said he also used the name, Quentin LeMonde.

"Do you remember anything at all he said to Pablo?"

"It was wadi-wadi, so I can come pretty close. It was something about a woman named Claire. He was to shut up about her, or something. Pablo said he had never said anything about her. He didn't talk about something or other, to anyone, at any time. I went on to the stall for fish and they talked a minute. The fellow didn't seem to be mad or anything. He just said it wasn't a good idea to speak about people like Claire.

"Oh, shit! I'm the one who's supposed to know something, aren't I?"

"It's more than possible," Clint agreed. "If you're the only one who met any of them. Maybe Pablo introduced some of you to others he met on the street or something?"

"Well, he introduced Mark and me to someone named Frank and someone named Eugene," Mike said. "Maria said some guy was a dangerous thief. I didn't hear his name, but he hung around a bar in Haiti, near the docks. He was a big black with dredlocks and a lot of gold chains."

"I heard the name. Claire Auber," Ann said. "We were at that place where we rented the boat to take us to the reefs, Matt. You remember?"

"The big black woman who spoke perfect French. I sort of remember her. She sat at a table in the back of that little bar on the docks all the time. I said hello to her one other time."

"What did she do there, do you know?" Clint asked.

They both shrugged. They said she wore loud clothes and talked very Jamaican, when she wasn't speaking the good French. She spoke wadi-wadi, or patois, as they called it, and fairly good English. Matt said he thought she sold tourist trinkets. The higher end things. Everyone seemed to respect her.

"Voodoo," Judi said. "She was a witch woman. She sold amulets and ju-jus to people. I'll bet Pablo was worried about a curse that she put on him, for some reason."

"The bruja said someone in our party has a follow spell on them. She can sense it," Lila offered. "She doesn't know which one. It isn't her spell."

"So. Was it Pablo ... no. She never met him. He was dead when you went there. It will be one or more of us. If we can find who, we can work it to our advantage," Clint said.

"You believe in those things?" Mike asked.

"That some of them work? Yes. That they're magic, not really."

They talked awhile longer, then went to bed. Clint would stay on watch for two hours, then Matt, then Obilio, then Mark. Mike said he would take a shift, but Clint said he wanted him fresh, in the morning.

They got up at dawn – to find Judi and Ann weren't in the house. Lila came to report that they were gone. She woke up and they weren't there, she woke Cori and ran to the men's room. There was no noise to wake her during the night. She hadn't gone to sleep until late, and had slept soundly. Cori came in, terrified. She hadn't heard or seen anything.

All of them spread out and carefully looked for anything. Maria had managed to leave the blue plastic bits. Clint knew Judi could probably think of something.

Mike found what looked like blood in several spots along what seemed to be an animal path toward the ravine. It wasn't a lot and was hard to see in the dawn light, but was more obvious as the sun brightened. He felt he was being watched. It was eerie. He acted like he didn't see anything and came back to the others.

They went, as a group. Obilio looked carefully at the blood and said it wasn't human blood. He thought it was chicken blood. It smelled a little like chicken. Lila had killed a chicken last night and had it slow-cooking all night. They bled it into a jar and used the blood as flavoring and for the minerals in it in the soup, when it was almost done.

"I think Judi or Ann found a way to leave a trail," Clint suggested. "She managed to grab that jar on the way out and will leave it in small dribbles along the path they took.

"I wonder when and how whoever managed to get them out while we were watching!"

"Very simple," Obilio answered. "They used a spell or something in the water or any of many other things that would make us sleep. Perhaps the monosleep. The brujas make it. You will sleep very soundly for perhaps half an hour or less and will not remember. She makes it because, sometimes, it is hard to sleep. We take a very little. When you are asleep, you do not awaken unless there is something. After."

"Wouldn't the women be asleep, too?" Mike asked.

"Yes. It took two very large men to carry them. They left little to indicate they were here," Lila offered.

"No. Judi wasn't asleep – or Ann. Someone left that trail. Someone was awake and alert enough to think of it and act," Clint pointed out. "I don't understand why she didn't do something to wake us."

"You know, if Pop or one of us was threatened, they wouldn't do anything that might get us killed," Mike said. "Maybe point a gun at one or all of us and warn that anything would make them shoot."

"I agree," Matt said. "Why weren't they asleep? The rest of us were."

"Those two were already in the bedroom. We all had a glass of that corn drink before we went to bed. I think we can test it, somehow, and it will have the stuff in it," Mark said. "Maybe Judi wasn't supposed to be awake, and it changed their plans a bit."

"Judi will find subtle ways to slow them down. We have to follow them, fast!" Clint ordered. "They're clever. They might be close. Maybe they don't think we can follow.

"Mike, you said you felt you were being watched by the path? Do you feel it now? At all?"

Mike nodded. "I sort of little nagging feeling."

"Then you go toward the finca, where Luis keeps the horses with Luis. The watching spell the bruja mentioned is probably on you. They'll depend on it to tell them where all of us are. We can use it to our own advantage. Mark will stay here, at the house, out of sight. They may come or may send someone to find something, here. Judi will know I'll expect that. She'll be able to make them think something is here. That will separate one of them, if there are more than one. It could make it a bit hairy for Judi and Ann, if there's only one ... no. They'll either be forced to come along, or locked in a house, or something.

"If someone comes, stay out of sight and note where they go. Follow them, if you can stay where they won't know. They'll lead us to the women, if we haven't found them before. If we find them, one of us will come back here before we do anything, if we have the time.

"Cori will go back with Mike and Luis. They can see that nothing happens to her ... and that she can't be held in danger to keep us away. (She started to protest. That made her understand that Clint wanted no way for her to be held hostage.) We'll all be packing. We might end up having to shoot our way out of something. If it comes to that, you shoot. This isn't a game or a TV show.

"Questions?"

They all agreed. Mike, Cori and Luis headed down the mountain, Mark, Obilio and Matt went with Clint to a near-by place, where the path couldn't be seen from anywhere else, and waited until they were a distance away before Mark went back to the house from behind. Clint was a hell of a lot more worried about Judi and Ann than he was about to let on.

Clint and Matt let Obilio do most of the tracking. The chicken blood trail ended after less than a kilometer, when they found the jar under some bushes by the trail. There were spots about every 100 meters along the way. There was still a lot of the blood in the jar. That worried Clint. Was she caught, or did she ditch the jar to keep from being caught?

They were going in the general direction of where they followed before. Obilio stopped them, after awhile, and said he was pretty sure he knew where they were hiding. They could get to the place by either path. It was about three kilometers along. Those two paths were the only way in or out. They would come close to the other path, but across the river, about half a kilometer ahead. The river was shallow and easy to cross, there, but the crosser would be very visible. He felt one of them should go to the other path, in case one of them saw them coming on this one. They would probably try to take the other path out, in that case.

Clint thought for a minute, then told Obilio and Matt to follow this path. He would cross the river a little farther back and would get to the other path. Give him fifteen minutes, then go ahead as they were going.

He went back to a spot where there were rocks all along in the river, just behind a bend that would hide him from the lower ford. He was able to cross without a lot of trouble, then went on through the brambles and shrubs to find the path. He moved along it for about two and a half kilometers, where he was starting to go through a little patch of tall grass when he heard a voice asking what the hell they thought they were doing. They would never get away with this crap!

It was Judi, acting scared and indignant. If there was one thing Clint knew about her, it was that she was *not* scared.

A voice hissed for her to shut up, or he would shut her up.

Clint checked his Glock, then started to move ahead, slowly, when a second male voice said something in French, with a strong accent. He stepped back and waited. A short time later, two men came into view, with Ann and Judi between them. They were very carefully scanning ahead and were moving slowly when they came out of the grass and to the easier and more visible path. They speeded up. One had a gun. He would be Quentin or whatever. The other was a big black with dredlocks. He had a machete in his hand and a pistol stuck in his belt. Clint waited until they passed and stepped out on the path when they were about twenty feet ahead. He quietly said that if either of them moved one step or acted in a manner that he would think maybe, just perhaps, they were going for a weapon, he would see that it was the last thing they ever did.

Quentin spun and snapped a shot very close to Clint. That gave Judi an opportunity to step close and do a kick, while moving toward him. He fell over backward, but held onto the pistol. The other one started to grab for the pistol in his belt. Clint dove forward and snapped a shot at him, then rolled and snapped one at Quentin. He yelled for Judi and Ann to head down that path, the way they had come, as fast as the could go. A bunch of people were coming from that direction.

They bolted. Judi kicked the big black in the head as she passed, which made him swear when he dropped the pistol. Quentin jumped up and was trying to draw a bead on Clint, who shot a bit wildly over his head, but he dodged the shot from Quentin and had to turn to get another shot. Clint was about to shoot him when the black grabbed him around the ankle – which saved his life. He went down as Quentin put a shot right where his head was a split second before.

Clint brought the butt of his pistol down on the black's head and rolled to the side as Quentin fired again, nicking him slightly in the left arm. He kept rolling and went over the side of the path and sprung to his feet to dodge through the brush. Quentin fired at the sounds of his rush, but wasn't very close. Judi and Ann would be beyond where they could go back after them. They didn't know how many or who were coming toward them from that direction. Clint heard them running along the path away from the direction they came from. By the time he reached the path again, they were gone.

There was some blood (besides his), so he had hit one of them. He wasn't about to go after them. They could hide and ambush him, where he wouldn't stand a chance of surviving.

About ten minutes later, Obilio came running along the path. He saw Clint and stopped, then was concerned because of the blood. Clint's. Clint shook his head and said it wasn't serious. He thought a minute. Obilio was quiet.

"Maria wasn't with them!" Clint exclaimed. "I'll be alright. It's just a small flesh wound.

"Are the women alright?"

"Only Judi and Ann are here, but they heard enough to know that Maria is being sent out of the country, somehow, and a man called Aurelio," Obilio replied. "I think she is still close. They had no time to take her anywhere. They would have been seen."

"Let's check where they were. Maybe there's something there that will tell us something."

They went back to a cave that was close to the intersection of the two paths. There were some clothes and food and three bedrolls.

"They held Maria here," Obilio said. "The bedroll is still here, so she hasn't been taken far. She is probably close and they did not want Judi or Ann to know."

"They didn't count on me," Judi said. "We were all supposed to be asleep with a potion they kept talking about that we would all have gotten. They said it never failed before. They couldn't understand it.

"I told them I know a little voodoo myself. It would automatically not work on me, and Ann was right there, beside me. I protected her by being close.

"I don't know why Ann and I didn't get it. Everyone else did, apparently. They do think maybe I have a little power. They believe in that power. Antoin is scared shitless of it."

"We figured it was in the chicha we had before we went to bed," Matt replied. "You two were in the kitchen, fixing the chicken.

"Whose idea was the blood? Why did you toss the jar?"

"It was Judi's idea. They were forcing us out, saying you were all helpless. they would shoot you, one at the time, if we gave them any trouble. Judi turned in the doorway and said something about turning off the stove. She went in. The jar was right there, beside the stove. It didn't register that it's a wood stove and isn't turned off," Ann said. "Antoin saw a couple of drops of the blood when he went back to check the trail behind and was telling Denis about it. I said none of us were bleeding. He was crazy! I got in their face and Judi threw the jar in the bushes when they were looking at me. They searched us and didn't find anything or anywhere we had cut ourselves to leave a trail. They decided it was some wounded animal's blood, but they watched our every step, from then on."

"Antoin didn't let Denis do anything to us. He said he wouldn't be part of hurting women," Judi said. "I think Maria will be alright, if we can find her. I also think I could have gotten to Antoin with the voodoo bit, if I had some time. Do the incantation thing and use some of that sleight of hand stuff I teach the kids at the school."

"Antoin didn't want to be any part of this," Ann agreed. "On the other hand, he talked about killing two men before he came to Panamá so they wouldn't tell something."

"What did they want from Ann?" Clint asked.

They shrugged. All they were asked was if they knew some people and what Ann and Cori had said to Claire. "They seemed to think we told her something about somebody, because of Maria, but they didn't say so, directly. Ann sort of pieced that out from remarks on the way here and what they asked."

"Claire seems to be behind whatever it is," Matt said.

"One thing is still scary," Judi warned. "I did hear them say that if Ann didn't know anything, it had to be Cori."

That was something to think about, certainly. Clint wondered if they would go after Cori, now. They had to find Maria. She would be the key. Obilio had been right that the three bedrolls would mean she was still somewhere close. Clint remembered the caves not too far back along the second trail, off of a sidepath. That could have been where they were headed when they had their little encounter. It was worth a try.

Judi fixed his arm with a clean bandage she found in a small first aid kit. She and Ann would go with Obilio, back to the house, then down to the farm, where Luis had taken Cori and Mike. Matt and Clint would go to the caves.

After the others were gone, Clint made plans with Matt. "They'll definitely have traps to warn them," Matt said. "I wish we had better knowledge about the area. We might have a way they wouldn't expect."

"I noticed the area from above when we came across that ledge, higher up," Clint replied. "If I remember, the caves were in the side of a kind of escarpment. We're damned limited as to access. We'll have to depend on distraction. It's better than fifty-fifty they're in those caves. We have no choice. We plan as we go."

Matt looked grim, and nodded. They headed along the trail toward the caves, being very careful. Clint insisted they carry the pistols in their hands and that no one hesitated to shoot, if things got too dangerous.

It took almost an hour to reach the cut-off to the caves. Clint suggested they go past a short way, to see if there was another approach. He said he didn't like it so quiet. The usual animal cries and bird calls had ceased a few minutes ago. He would think it was them and would be a good warning that they were on the way, but Matt said the calls were there all along, until now. The only ones that stopped were the ones directly on the path and in sight. The parrots were even noisier when they passed. Now they were quiet.

"It's the time of day they're going to roost," Clint noted. "They were noisiest when they flew over. This is eerie – that the noises have so completely stopped. I can't figure why. Unless it's something they've done they have to be damned nervous about it."

There was a far-off rumbling sound, followed by a slight tremor. A few seconds later, there was a smaller aftershock.

"Tremor. Animals and birds sense them, or hear them forming, or something," Matt said. "We have an explanation for us. I wonder if our targets know about that."

"Maybe it can work to our advantage, if my luck's done a one eighty," Clint agreed. "If things are normal, it will make them even more paranoid."

They went on for a few hundred meters, then went off the side of the path along a fallen tree to the more easily navigated shade under the thick canopy. The lack of light made it easy to move. Not much grew in the dense shade. They were able to move to a point only about two hundred meters from the caves. The big black was sitting in front of one, with a rifle standing beside him, leaned against the side of a large boulder. Clint pointed to a spot with dense foliage a bit below, when someone inside the cave screamed.

"Let's rumble!" Matt said, and ran into sight. Clint drew a bead on Antoin, who started to reach for the rifle, but stopped. "I won't help him when he hurts a woman, Mon," he said.

Matt went to the mouth of the cave, there was a sudden shot, and he dropped. Clint ran from the side and snapped a shot into the cave mouth, where he saw movement. There was a sharp grunt and a scrambling noise.

"I'm not hit," Matt said. "I saw him move."

Antoin said he was leaving. He didn't mean to ever get involved in something that meant they would kidnap women. They knew he was like that when they sent him.

"Claire?" Matt asked. He nodded.

"You have five minutes before I come after you. If

Maria isn't hurt, I'll take longer," from Matt.

"I have nothing to do with hurting no woman, Mon. Nothing." He grabbed a backpack from just inside the cave mouth and started down the trail toward the river. He left the rifle there.

"That should be time enough for Denis to get out the back way. We can hope Maria isn't hurt. Let's get her."

They went inside, to find a large boulder blocking the passage into the cave. They started for the front and an even larger one dropped across the opening. It was dark inside, and getting dark outside.

"Shit!" Matt cried.

"That about covers it," Clint agreed.

Clint used the light from his cell phone to search around the cave a bit. They could move the boulder in back enough to get through, so concentrated on that. The rocks had apparently been balanced by using poles as levers to roll them up enough that dropping a stay, probably a smaller rock, would drop them to seal the entrances. They should be easy to roll away far enough to let them get through, but the one in the front entrance had a couple of rocks shoved against and partly under, after it was in place. That acted as a chock that wouldn't allow it to move. The rear entrance wasn't chocked. Denis was probably hurt enough to where he couldn't manage the smaller chocks. That meant Antoin had suckered them. He had to be the one who chocked the one in front – or there was a third person involved.

"It's a good thing we could move that thing," Matt said. "If they had put something there to stop it, we would be in deep trouble."

"Obilio would have come, if we weren't back soon," Clint replied. "I wasn't worried about that. I'm just pissed that we let Antoin con us."

"I don't think it was Antoin. The rifle's still there."

Clint picked up the old Enfield and checked it over. It seemed to be in good shape.

They headed back toward Obilio's place. He, Luis, and Mike were coming to look for them. They were walking back to Obilio's when Clint stopped to think for a minute, then swore.

"What?" from Matt.

"If you were being held and your captors kidnaped then two other women, would you ... something isn't adding up here. Not even close."

"I wondered," Obilio replied. "I wondered why Maria was gone, fighting against someone who had killed her husband, had time to scream one time from behind the bodega, but didn't make any other noise. She didn't do anything to help us find her. She put little pieces of blue plastic on plants for us to find, but couldn't make a better trail or make some noise? Judi dropped blood and broke little branches. Why didn't *she* break some branches? She was free enough to place the plastic pieces. She had time enough to push the twigs through the plastic, but always just a little to the side of the path, not right on it.

"I have thought on this. It does not make any sense. It is like the clues in a movie or TV show.

"There is much to know about that one. If someone killed me in front of Lila, they would have to kill her, right then and there. The same as if someone hurt her. I would die very loud while trying to kill them. I would not be quiet and walk off to the side of a path to hang little pieces of plastic on bushes. I would not be quiet for anyone to take me anywhere.

"Also, who was in the house where the chicha was fermenting? Who knew Ann would not drink it?

"Yes, amigo. We need to have some answers to a large number of questions."

They all agreed with that statement.

"I have to talk with the bruja!" Clint suddenly said. Mike looked thoughtful, then nodded. He was very bright and practical for his age.

They went back to the house. Clint said there would be two watching, at all times. They weren't to eat or drink anything there that could have been tampered with. They also had to find out what the hell was going on!

In the morning Clint, Matt, and Obilio went to the bruja's house. She was reluctant to say anything until Clint said he knew very well that Maria was also a bruja. She didn't have the power to do this. She was working for someone else. Probably Claire Auber.

When Clint said "Claire Auber," the bruja flinched noticeably.

"Okay. All we have to know is what this is about. No other questions will be asked, now."

"You can't fight her. She is very strong. She sent ... things to prove her power. I am an old woman who only knows medicine. I have a sense of some things. There is a follow spell on one of you. Not one here now. It does nothing else, but it is very good. It is strong enough that I can't block it."

"Do you know why this is happening?" Obilio asked.

"One of you has knowledge of something that is very dangerous to a person in Haita. It must be known what will be done with the information, if it is not stopped."

"Nothing would have been done with it, before they started attacking us," Matt said. "We don't even know what it's about."

She looked thoughtful. She said she would relay that information. Maybe those evil people would go away.

"One has died. Just now. This moment."

"By natural causes?" Clint asked.

"No." She refused to say more. Clint thanked her, They went back to the house, where Clint insisted the women go to David and that they don't go anywhere, except as a group. He told Judi what they had learned and believed.

"Judi, Maria will probably try to contact you. Don't."

Judi knew what he meant. She nodded agreement.

They went as a group to the carretera. They stayed

together until the women were all on the bus. Obilio insisted Lila go with them. Clint called his nutty musician friend, Dave, and asked if he could use his house in Quiteño. Dave was in Panamá City, but said the key was where Clint knew. Make themselves at home.

When the bus was gone, the men went back to Obilio's house. Mike asked why.

"So they can contact us," Mike said.

"And to sit here until we can figure out what it is that Ann or Cori knows," Clint added. "I also want to know if it's Denis or Antoin who's dead, all of a sudden."

"I think it will be Antoin. I think he'll have died much the same way Pablo died."

Clint nodded. Antoin had refused to follow orders.

They tried to think of anything that might have a bearing on this mess. Who did Ann or Cori know something about? What kind of thing was it? Maria was still the point where everything came together. She was on the other side, but was the center point. When did they meet her? Under what circumstances? Who else was she seen with?

"I doubt we were around when whatever was told to or seen by Ann or Cori," Mike said. "We'd be in the same kind of mess as they are.

"Maria. I first met her when we were at that little restaurant where they had the stewed conch we liked, remember? She waited on us. It was the only time I ever saw her around the place. We ate there two or three times a week, sometimes all of us, and, most times, one or two of us. I ate there three times a week. Pablo worked in the kitchen. I had seen him in there, most times I went.

"I think, if we check, they weren't married, huh?"

Clint nodded. "That was where you all met her?"

They agreed, but didn't know if Ann or Cori had seen her before. Clint called Judi, but they were on the bus and weren't in range of a relay. It would have to wait.

"We have to work on the times before that when Ann or Cori were out to meet anyone," Matt said. "We don't stay too close after we're in a place a couple of days to learn how to get around and where to go. We met her after about four days of that. It's in a pretty restricted time. We didn't ... I wonder!"

"Wonder?" Clint asked.

"I seem to remember Cori saying she thought she had seen Maria, once, in Jamaica. It was later, after we met at the restaurant. Cori said it was either her or a sister or something such. Mike said a lot of those people look a lot alike. They're pretty much inbred, on those islands."

"I remember saying that, but don't remember why I said it," Mike said. "It might have been ... we weren't apart so much in Jamaica. We only stayed there three days. It had to be that last night, when Cori went to that club with that LeBonne guy. The one I said was a stereotypical French gigolo. You said Cori knew how to handle the type, Mark. Remember?"

"Emile LeBonne. I remember. I thought it was funny. He's about thirty and Cori's sixteen. She can handle that type. I guess that would be the only time it could have been and the only one it could have been. Cori. In Jamaica. We have to concentrate on what happened in Jamaica, not Haiti.

"Claire Auber is in Haiti, but those people move around all the time, anyhow."

"Yeah. She might be working for anyone," Clint agreed. "I think maybe I'll go to David. I want to have a long remembrance session with Cori. She knows something that's deadly to her, meaning it's as deadly to somebody else.

"Would the club she went to be a place drug importers would go?"

They shrugged. Mike said he doubted it had anything to do with drugs. It was something else.

They decided that Clint could sneak away when it was unlikely anyone would know. He could go to the other side of the next mountain and get a ride from the village there into David. Obilio would arrange it. Obilio put the flag up, with a single black stripe down the middle. Luis would bring one horse and would ride with Clint to where he could find the path out. He would go most of the way. He would bring the horse back.

Clint packed a few things and headed out, as soon as Luis arrived.

Clint watched the house for awhile from across the campo. Judi came out a few times, but Ann and Cori stayed inside. Lila did what almost any Indigeno woman would do if they were staying in someone's house. She cleaned the place better than it had ever been cleaned before. She had laundry out and went to the market on the corner of the main road to bring back lots of food. Judi paid for it, but stayed with Ann and Cori.

Just after dark Clint called and told Judi he was across the campo and would stay there at Gringo Bill's place, where he could see if anybody came around who wasn't part of the local population.

Judi said she had three perdidos (phone calls where the caller hung up before you can answer, the object being that you call back and pay for the conversation) since they left Obilio's. She didn't answer, but noted they were from a private number. She couldn't call back if she wanted. She guessed someone was trying to find where they were.

"They know exactly where you are. The bruja said the follower spell wasn't one of us there. We were all there, except you four. It won't be Lila or you. It could be Ann or Cori. I'd say Ann."

Clint told her to answer, if anyone called. He fully expected someone to try to contact them. He said he had to talk with Cori. It was her who they were after. They had figured part of it. Tell her to concentrate on remembering Jamaica and going to a club with Emile. He would call later to arrange for a meeting. Dave had the house as secure as anyplace around. Lock all the deadbolts before they went to bed.

After the call, Clint watched the house. He could stay in the window of Bill's place and not sleep all night, if he felt it was necessary.

He got a call from Obilio. Antoin's body was found near the carretera. He was slashed up worse than Pablo had been. "I think you should be very extra careful if that witch woman is about. Do not let her get close enough to reach you. It is more important for the women."

Clint said, if she showed up at the house during the night and looked like she was trying to get in, she was going to have a heart attack. Her heart was going to be attacked by a few ounces of brass jacketed lead.

Nothing happened that night. Clint figured they would know he was gone from Obilio's by now, so went to the house for breakfast. After the hojaldras, eggs, and bolitas he took Cori across to the bench at the campo and started asking about Jamaica.

"Well, I went with Emile – he wasn't as bad as Mike and Dad thought, but that's still not a prize – to a sort of private club, where the rich and infamous go. It was so plush it could make you puke, all artificial wood crud. The bar had all the expensive crap. I had a Tanqueray and tonic that I sipped for an hour or so. Emile introduced me to a lot of people. Juan Peso, from Mexico – he owns a bunch of hotels. Carlos Vermont, from Nicaragua, owns some kind of resort on the lake. Gino Spellini, from Italy who owns a big casino in Panamá City.

"I don't remember all of them. Fred Something, from the US and Sean Carmichael, from Canada – he's some kind of liaison. Hermanito Ortega, from Colombia. He's government, too. Lou Fontenac, from Jamaica ... a lot of politicians from everywhere. A German liaison officer named Marks, an Israeli called Solomon. Even some Smythe character from Merry Old. Gino Garibaldi, from Italy. Achilles Aphel-something, from Greece, even. Mike Partridge, from Australia. Some woman from Guatemala and somebody from Venezuela and somebody from Argentina and a really hot woman from Brazil and a really fat man from Ecuador. Enrique Something.

"Emile was trying to impress me with all the bigshit politicians and rich sons of bitches he knew. Nobody stands especially out, except the Smythe asshole. He kept hitting on me. He thought I was eighteen. I told them that, but nobody really cared, except the ones from the states and Canada and like that.

"I mean, all the Latins will hit on you. Sort of what's expected. They don't paw you like that pig. I'm blonde, so Latins react like I'm some Playboy bunny or something. I'm not a sexy bombshell, I'm rather ordinary.

"I notice the fair men from everywhere else will hit on the fiery dark exotic Latina. Some of them are so sexy they turn me on! Those Latino guys ignore them! I guess it's what you're used to. I couldn't point to any one of them and say there might be something there. They were just a bunch of politicians and casino and hotel owners at a party."

Clint thought for a minute, then nodded. "I think I see what it is. It's not that he or she was there, it's that they were there."

"They who?"

"That's what I have to find out."

"You're weird. In a kind of neat way, but weird!"

"Wait 'til you meet Dave, who owns the house you're staying in."

"Judi told us about him. He's just a musician and a writer. They're all weird."

They chatted awhile. Cori was as bright and mentally older as her younger brother.

Clint had a direction, of sorts. He knew what he had to learn.

Which ones at that party were definitely not supposed to be at that party – and why?

"Clint, I got a call from someone who claims to only be a neutral party who wants to settle the disagreement between the Campbells and some people on the Caribbean Islands," Judi said, when she called Clint, in the morning. Clint had gone into David and was staying at the Pensión Costa Rica. "I told him any deals were with you, not me and not the Campbells."

"What did he say to that?"

"That you were never concerned. It was an accident that you and I got involved, at all."

"And?"

"I said that Pablo was murdered in cold blood on the property of a friend of yours, you were shot, I was abducted – and we aren't involved? How droll!"

"That sounds like you. What next?"

"He said he doesn't know about any of that. He wasn't told. He was simply getting in touch with us because a person involved discovered you were with the Campbells."

"Yeah. Right."

"He'll call you. He said for me to arrange something. I gave him your number and said to call you."

"Thanks. Take care. This is as weird as what else has happened."

They chatted a moment, then Clint hung up. He could figure about how long it would take for whoever to call him. If he really wasn't involved on that end, he would have to check it out.

Clint was up all night. It would be very soon, if this turkey was involved. It would take several hours, if he wasn't. If he wasn't, Clint could get some information from him.

It was three and a half hours later when the call came. Chances were this guy wasn't too deeply involved. He was trying to deliver a message and to defuse the situation, as he claimed. Clint would meet him at the Alcalá restaurant at six. He would see what was up, then. He might be up all night again, so he got another three hours of sleep, then went to the Alcalá and into the restaurant. He got a table and was there about ten minutes when a dark bullish man came to sit across the table from him. He quickly introduced himself as Oscar Mittermann. Major Oscar Mittermann, if it made a difference.

"Not to me. What do you want?"

"I've checked on you. I know more about you right now than you do, probably. I think we can work together.

"What is going on, quite frankly, is that a bunch of people from various countries are planning some kind of weird mutual action to consolidate military forces to challenge the US about some operations. We can't let that happen. At the same time, we can't let the people know we have anything on them or their plot."

"You can't make a dent in the drug trade with the methods you're using. Everyone here knows how false your wolf cries are. Ever since Ollie North, your programs are a joke."

"Don't I know it! It has nothing to do with drugs. I've got better ways to waste my time. These people are planning to take control of the canal and shipping to and from most of the South and Central American countries."

"Can't happen. The canal isn't defendable. The US is their major market. Try again."

Mittermann studied him a minute. Clint called the waiter over and ordered a thick pork steak with all the trimmings, then sat back. Mittermann ordered the same and grinned at Clint.

"It's about ... this is going to sound stupid ... voodoo. A group from Haiti and Jamaica are scaring the hell out of the pols in several of these countries. They want to run things.

"Okay. That's true, but they're backed, sponsored, by a ... this sounds like crap."

"It is crap. Why are you doing this? Insulting my intelligence isn't going to get any cooperation from me."

Mittermann sat back and got more and more nervous. "You know all the conspiracy theories going around, of course. They're more and more popular as people get more and more frustrated with big government and big money running it. Is it any easier to believe the truth? It's a scheme by a bunch of bankers to destroy the Federal Reserve and impose a currency on all the South and Central American countries – that they control.

"Maybe there's a conspiracy in the states and Europe, maybe not. I tend to think there is, frankly. I just don't have a clue about how to fight it. They have the power."

"I could agree with dumping the Fed," Clint agreed. "That's where one hell of a lot of the world's problems are coming from. I could agree with a currency among all the countries in the Americas – *if* the Fed wasn't in control. If they set something up like you suggest, it's the same thing here. If it's true, I wouldn't blink to learn that the US Fed's behind it. We need a universal exchange. We don't need that bunch in control of it. It's the end of economic freedom for anyone.

"I listen to a lot of the stuff. I agree with some of it and disagree with some of it. I'm not sure the cure isn't worse than the disease, though.

"I don't give a shit about it. I can be with the Indios. I won't be affected. When you or anyone else brings it to them, you have me to fight."

"I swear to you on whatever oath you care to impose that we didn't know about Armand Gault and that bunch. We knew that Claire Auber has her thumb in it up to the elbow. We could have figured it would get out of hand. Hope she doesn't decide to come here. She has all the witch doctors in this hemisphere scared shitless of her. Voodoo is involved, to that extent. Too many of the bigshits believe in that garbage."

"I've seen a few things. Some of it works, but I don't believe magic is involved."

"They're very able with untraceable poisons and such methods."

"Among other things. Maybe some few of them have some minor psy power, or something. The bruja on the comarca can sense the follower spell Auber put on one of the women. That works."

Mittermann stared at Clint a moment. He didn't know if he was serious, so he said he was. He didn't have a clue to how it worked.

"Oh? She knows who has the spell, or that one of them does?" Mittermann asked.

"That one or more of them have it. That it's the women. All the men were with me when we talked with her. She knew it wasn't them."

"She senses electrical emanations, somehow. We have a few in the department who can do that. They're sensitive. There will be some kind of device involved. Those people can get their hands on almost any of the crap."

"Then we can find it," Clint said.

"Yeah. We can get a wideband scanner and find it."

"Do that and I'll help – if just to get the type who brought this to the Indios out of here."

Mittermann didn't say anything. He made a call on a somewhat large cell phone, then said a man would meet them in one hour in the parque. He would have the bugchaser, as they called it.

Clint and Mittermann had the delicious meal and chatted, then went to the parque, where a bum came to sell them contraband CDs and DVDs. Mittermann looked through his cooler of CDs and bought three. The bum put them in a bolsa and slipped a package in, took the five dollars, and latched onto a passing gringo, saying he had all the latest CDs and DVDs from the states. Just a dollar apiece!

Clint and Mittermann went to Peter's place and had a Balboa, then went out to take a cab that happened to be passing. The CD salesman was the driver. They went to Quiteño and used the bugchaser. There was one transponder in Ann's purse, made into the clasp. She said she bought it in Haiti from a stand on the street. She didn't know how they could know it was her who would buy it.

"They didn't," Judi said. "They saw which one it was and substituted when you were out, or something."

Cori also had one. It was in a necklace she bought in Haiti.

"Okay. I'm convinced I can work with you, but I don't believe one word of the crap explanation," Clint said.

"Fair enough," Mittermann replied. "I'll take you back to the Costa Rica and meet with you tomorrow. We can figure some angle. I'm with you about getting those kinds out of here."

He dropped Clint off. The taxi took him on to his hotel, the Alcalá. Clint went inside the Costa Rica, talked with the owner, Lee, and Bob for awhile, then went to his room..

That was successful! Now to find out who Armand Gault was and what was really going on.

He called Judi and warned her Mittermann had probably put some kind of fancy spy device there, so be careful. She said Cori was watching him in the mirror from the bathroom when he slipped a cute little thing behind the toilet. They checked and found one behind the refrigerator and another in the master bedroom.

"And one under the server shelf to the kitchen from the sala," Clint said. "I saw that one. He wasn't too subtle. I was probably expected to be watching and wouldn't know he planted others. Pick them all up, say goodnight into them and go to bed. There're probably more of different kinds. I suppose they're listening to this.

"You people need new methods. TV's already exposed all of this. If we knew anything, we'd be damned sure you wouldn't learn about it, unless we decide there's a reason you should know. This just means we won't trust any of you an inch. You have, as they say here, shot yourself in the ass.

"See you tomorrow, Jude. Tell everybody good night for me."

They hung up. Clint went to bed.

"Good morning, Clint!" Clint heard, when he answered the phone. He was sitting in the little open-air restaurant across from the taxi stand by Romero's. It was ten to six. Not much else was open in David.

"Good morning," he replied. "Mike?"

"Uh-huh. We caught some crud sneaking around by

the bodega. Obilio decided that, seeing he's so interested in it, we would lock him in until you come to ask him a number of polite questions."

"What does he say?"

"Nothing, except that he's with the US government and is here to protect us. He said to call you and to have you talk to somebody called Oscar."

"No. He's from the CIA and isn't there to protect anybody. You shouldn't need any protection, but ... you might. Tell him to let you know what he's looking for and maybe you'll help him find it. I'll call Oscar and let him know how much we appreciate all this crap.

"I think the most dangerous one, where we're concerned, is the witch woman, Claire. I haven't a clue as to what they're doing. The explanations don't make sense. All I know is that they're doing something that will ... I'll be damned!"

"What?"

"You know something? I think we're being used as a distraction. Cori happened to be at a place at a time that ... That makes no sense, either. It's too complicated to have a hope it will work. Antoin wouldn't be dead, if that was it.

"Christ! I can't make anything make sense! I suppose you can let your guest go. There will be someone from the other side lurking around. Be careful. If there's any kind of attack, shoot to kill."

"We already decided that. Call after you talk to that Oscar character. We'll keep this one on ice until we hear from you."

Clint agreed, and hung up. The phone buzzed almost immediately. "We don't have anybody out there! Don't let him go!" Mittermann almost screamed.

"Good morning. You can get a car that can get us there

fairly fast?"

"Is there a place a chopper can land?"

"A small one."

"Airport. Fifteen minutes." He hung up.

What in HELL is going on? Clint thought, as he dropped some money on the counter and flagged a taxi from across the street. He was at the airport eight minutes and twenty dollars later. He told the cabbie there was twenty in it if he was there in less than ten minutes. He was. Mittermann came about five minutes later and they went to the private chopper sitting near the terminal building. They were landing on Obilio's mountaintop nine and a half minutes later. On the way, Clint told Mittermann one more lie and the cooperation was gone for good. He had no authority in Panamá. This turkey was Obilio's capture, on the comarca, and Obilio would decide who and when anyone else spoke to him. Mittermann said the sad fact was that they were trained to never tell the truth about anything.

"That's your reputation. This guy said to talk to you."

"So connect the dots, but it's from the wrong direction. Mike said he wanted you to talk to Oscar. Nobody in the outfit or out calls me Oscar. It's always Mittermann."

Clint nodded. He said that was what make him suspicious, from the first. What was the object?

"You almost did it. You almost said to let him go. By the time you found out he wasn't from the agency, he'd be in Paris or somewhere."

"Port au Prince."

"I don't think he's with them. I really don't. We've identified all of them who are here. That scares me."

Clint was surprised. He said they would find out who he was with. Mittermann said he would be trained against telling them anything true. He wouldn't react to pain.

"We have an expert on making people talk," Clint said.

"I think it won't work. We have everything, and we have counters for everything. Built in."

"You just think you do. You greatly underestimate the resources on the comarca. You underestimate these people – again."

Mittermann grinned. "You know something? I think maybe you can get answers."

Mike and Obilio came out to the chopper. Mark and Matt were inside. They had rifles pointed at anyone who got off the chopper they didn't know, already. Obilio pointed to the bodega and said someone tried to come to it from in back. A couple of shots that missed less than an inch seemed to have convinced him that wasn't a good idea. It was too dark to see much of anything about him.

Obilio took the heavy board holding the door shut off, and opened the door.

"Armand?! In person!?" Mittermann cried, almost screeched.

"Hello, Mittermann. It would seem these people are better at this kind of thing than either of us."

"Shall we go to the house and have some hot strong coffee?" Obilio suggested.

Clint laughed, then Mittermann, then Armand.

"Might as well be civilized about it," Armand said. "Armand Gault. You're Clint Faraday. I know who the Campbells are."

"Obilio, comarca councilman and area boss," Mike introduced. "This shit gets weirder and weirder!"

"You can say that again," Mittermann said.

"This shit gets weirder and weirder." Mike said, looking innocent. Mittermann giggled, and waved at the house.

There was a shot from above them in the forest. Gault staggered and dropped.

Matt stepped out of the house and scanned the area with binoculars, then carefully shot at a spot in the forest.

"Probably didn't hit, but it will be close. There was a spot of smoke from that shot."

Gault had crawled a few feet to a large rock that Lila had planted terstrial orchids around. He sat up and swore steadily. There was blood coming from his right shoulder.

"Come on!" Mittermann said. "You've been shot before!"

"Asshole!" Gault said. He stood, unsteadily.

Matt was watching the spot where he'd shot through the binoculars. He grunted and said someone was running through the meadow toward the path they had followed already, two times. He waited another few seconds, then said, "Damn! It's Maria!"

That really got Gault to swearing.

"You were working for her, huh?" Clint asked.

"*With* her, I thought. Bitch!"

They went into the house. Mittermann made a bandage for Gault's arm. He said they would have to get him to a hospital.

"After while," Clint said.

"It could be critical. I can't stop the bleeding."

"Then it would be wise for Mr. Gault to answer Clint's questions quickly," Obilio said. "You may not leave the comarca until I say you may leave the comarca."

"I think Armand has a stong incentive to answer the questions," Mittermann said.

"Ask away," Gault said.

"Who and what?" Clint asked.

"A group. To establish a control of banking in Central and South America, including all the islands in the gulf and Caribbean."

"You're part of the group?"

"Apparently not. I thought I was."

"Maria is. That's obvious."

"No. She is a sociopath who's being used by a woman known as Claire Auber. Claire Auber is one of the twelve people who are running things. Eleven. I'm obviously going to do what I can to end them. Dr. Freud would make a big case study of someone like her!"

"Maria's a sociopath who may have been acting on her own," Mittermann pointed out.

"Or not," he replied. "I'll cooperate. I don't know if you can do anything, if Auber is behind it."

"Oh, I can," Clint said. "Obilio, I think we can allow Mr. Gault leave to go to a hospital."

Obilio nodded. Mittermann took Gault to the chopper. They took off. Clint would have to stay. The chopper was a two-seater.

"Why did you not ask him what he came here to find?" Obilio asked.

"I caught that," Mike said. "Good question!"

"Because I want to find it." Clint went to the bodega. They took everything out. Obilio said it was a good time to clean the place. He cleaned everything and they put most of it back. They didn't find anything.

"Gault and Maria think it's here. Maria was here. Whatever it is has to be here," Clint said, stubbornly. "It wouldn't make sense that she would go to that trouble to find something she ... so we locked Gault up in this bodega. Damn! How stupid!"

"I think he did not take anything away with him," Obilio said. "I assure you, I would have found it when we made the bandages. I know how to find anything on a person."

"Then it's still right here. It's why he was so unconcerned when everything happened," Mike said. "He seemed a little bit smug to me the whole time."

"There wasn't any time since we let him out that he could have hidden anything," Mark argued. "He hid it somewhere in the bodega. It'll be a paper or something small. He slipped it under a floor ... there aren't any. It's a stone floor. It's under a stone."

"No stone was moved. I would know," Obilio said, positively.

Clint laughed. "I wonder, why did he crawl around after he was shot, when none of us were concentrating on him? Hmm? Want to bet?"

They went to search along the six feet Gault had crawled. Clint searched among the orchids and around the rock. He found a small plastic bag with a couple of sheets of paper in it. It was shoved under the rock behind a large sobralia, with a little bit of dirt piled on top. The sheets contained a number code. It would take some decoding – If Clint could find a base for the code.

"This means he'll be back," Matt said. "We can jump out and yell surprise!"

"I think he'll feel safe enough that he won't come, unless he knows none of us are here. He can wait," Mike suggested. "Maybe we should all go to David for a couple of days?"

"The helicopter is returning, now. Clint will be expected to go," Obilio said. "We can take the horses and go to David this afternoon, when Clint will already be there."

"But Clint will not be there after all of you arrive and we're seen putting the girls on the bus for Bocas," Clint said. "How wonderful! *All* of us went to Bocas! We even had a special bus, a privado, to take us!"

"He'll be watching," Mike warned. "Is there somewhere you can get off that he won't be able to know about?"

"Yo!"

"Should we inform your Mr. Mittermann of our plan?" Obilio asked.

"I'll decide on the way to David," Clint replied. "I don't trust any CIA agent. If he's being straight with us, I'll be straight with him. Otherwise...."

Mittermann landed the chopper, and came out to ask, "Did you find it? He damned well didn't have anything on him when we landed in David. He said he didn't find anything here, that he was looking for an item that Maria had left, by accident, but didn't find anything."

He looked at the bodega. Clint shook his head very

slightly at the others.

"We took the place apart, literally," Mike explained. "Whatever, it definitely ain't in that bodega."

"Damn! He couldn't have gotten rid of it since we let him out! Even in the house, there wasn't a second I didn't have him in view."

"That leaves one time. When he was shot and we were looking at the mountain, over there."

"You can look, but we thought of that," Mike said. Clint liked the way he told the exact truth, but left out a small detail or two.

He went carefully along to the rock garden, then searched around the rock. "It looks like something was dug up ... but that could be from the flower bed. There's nothing there now. Shit!"

"Maria!" Mark cried. "I'll be dog-damned! She was watching him through the scope and saw him hide it! She could have come back and got whatever it was! You think?"

"How could she?" Matt asked, innocently. "We were right there, in the house."

"Or all of us in the bodega, taking it apart and making a lot of noise?" Mark asked. "As Mittermann said, shit!"

"You were watching her running across the meadow over there," Mittermann pointed out.

"Half a minute or more after the shot and he dropped," Clint said. "There was time for something like that. Maybe after she crossed the meadow. No one could see her, then. A quick look to see he was against the rock."

"Shit!" from Mittermann and Mike, at the same time.

"We might as well go back to David. Obilio will have the Indios watch for Maria and to call him, if she's seen. She seems good at staying out of sight," Clint suggested. "I hope this will let the Campbells out of it.

They simply don't know anything."

Mittermann nodded. Matt said they would come to David in an hour or two. They would go back to Bocas. Obilio said he and Lila would go with them, if they would allow. Clint said he and the women would go. He'd arrange a private bus. They were out of it. It was Mittermann's headache, now. Mittermann seemed relieved. He said he thought there was no further danger to any of them – except, be careful of Maria. She was nuts.

Clint got in the chopper and Mittermann took him to David. They didn't talk much on the trip. When he got there, he went to the pensión to pack up his stuff. He talked a bit with Lee and Bob, then went to the terminal, where the bus he ordered was waiting. After that was settled and ready, he went to several places to ask some innocent questions and to leave copies of the coded sheets with a friend.. He managed to be back at the terminal when the bus came with Obilio and company. He called Judi. She said they would get there in twenty minutes. They would get to Bocas after dark, but them's the breaks. She had called Bocas. The Campbells would stay at the Bahia.

Obilio got a call as they were leaving the terminal to say that Maria was seen near the road. She may have left the area. Obilio said the reason she was there was gone.

There was a woman Clint had noted before on the comarca near the bus stop, sitting in front of the restaurant at La Mina. It was logical they would stop at the restaurant, there, considering the time they left David. The next stop was Punta Peña. That was two hours.

Clint and the men went into the restaurant before the women to order food for them all. Clint had a beer, as did Matt and Mike. They walked around a bit, while the women took a bit long to eat (as arranged). When they got back on the bus, the woman just happened to be selling empanadas and tamales. She stepped into the bus just before it left, but the driver said it was private. She knew she couldn't go onto a private bus to sell anything.

She didn't argue. She stepped back off. She had seen that they were all there.

The bus left. It was followed at a short distance by a small truck. Just before the divide (Quijada Diablo) the truck pulled off the road and turned around. Just past the divide, Clint got off the bus and it continued on. Clint went back a short way, then down a path past Gabriel's place and to the town of La Mina. There was a horse left there by a friend of Luis. It was a long trip to Obilio's, but no one could get there faster. Clint had a friend on the other side of the valley who would drive him to the comarca on the back road.

It took four hours to get there. Clint went up the path, carefully, and arrived at the house. Nobody had been there, from front or back. Clint knew how to make a trap that someone who knew methods would find. They would trip the real trap going around those.

Clint went back to the house to wait. He didn't expect anything until dawn, and there wasn't anything. Then a chopper came. He had ridden in that chopper. He hid and watched as Mittermann and Gault went to the rock to check, carefully. Mittermann and Gault were speaking French, but Clint knew enough to know that Mittermann was telling Gault that he figured Maria had gotten it. Gault swore very colorfully about something on his computer, then they got in the chopper and left.

Clint was very satisfied that he hadn't told Mittermann anything. He would have to find just how deeply

Mittermann was involved. He may be playing both ends.

Clint checked once more. He was about to leave when he heard something out back. He slipped behind the door to the second bedroom. Maria came in the window in back to look around the kitchen. She had a silly grin on her face as she went to the small cupboard, where the rice and dishes were kept. Clint made a noise, by throwing a shoe toward the front of the house, just as she was starting to move things. She quietly closed the cupboard and slipped back out the little window. Clint moved to the main door and came into the room, that way. He took out his Glock, checked it, and moved toward the bedrooms. He went in the first one and went to look out the window, studying the area. He then went toward the second bedroom. Maria would have to get back to the forest to wait for him to leave.

He went to the cupboard, searched around until he found two sheets that looked much like the two he had. He remembered enough to know the number code was different in a few spots than the two he had. He took out his notepad and wrote, *Tu siempre falta una cosa. Esta medio intelligente. G* and put it where the sheets had been secreted. He then puttered around for a while, then stepped outside to scan the sky, checked his watch, closed the house, and walked off down the path. He stopped just past the forest end of the path, where he could be seen from above the house. Maria would be there. He acted as though he was waiting for someone. After another half hour, he went back toward the house a little, then turned and went to Luis' friend's place. He got a horse he would leave with Luis. He left the horse and asked Luis to see if it would be possible to detain Maria for one day. Luis said this was the comarca. He could detain her for one century, if he chose.

Clint said she was a homicidal maniac. It wasn't important enough to take chances. Luis nodded and looked grim.

Clint took the bus to the airport and got a seat on the plane to Bocas. Judi would have made it seem he was there, to a watcher. He arrived with a small disguise on that made him look shorter and fatter than he was. He went to Judi's in a taxi and swam across to his deck. He was home for about fifteen minutes, Judi had brought over supper, when the phone buzzed. He answered.

"Clint? Mittermann. I've been busy, but wanted to see that your bunch got to Bocas Town safely."

"Yeah. We got here just a little before midnight. We stayed in Changuinola last night and came to Bocas on the first water taxi. I crashed for most of the day. You can ask Judi if anything else happened."

Before Mittermann could answer, Clint handed the phone to Judi. She chatted a minute about how the whole bunch were tired, except her and Mike. She could sleep on the bus, Mike could sleep on the bus, but none of the others could. Clint and Matt drank beer and talked. The others said they hadn't slept at all when they reached Changuinola. It was almost two before they found a hotel, then got up before dawn to get to Bocas. It was always good to get home.

Had he learned anything else?

This was an act to make him believe Clint was really there the whole time. Judi had been plenty visible. He knew damned well she was there. If Clint simply handed her the phone, he had been there all day.

Clint could picture him steaming while he had to sound totally unconcerned about anything. He said Gault said there was some kind of package left that was gone, but he couldn't find out what. Gault was in the hospital until the wound was stitched, or something.

Judi finally let him go. She laughed a bit about sounding like a chatty airhead, while he was trying to come up with an excuse to hang up.

Clint took the sheets and copied them, then hid the originals with the first two sheets. He noted the differences, which seemed to be on a list that was headed and followed by paragraphs.

Somebody cooking the books?

If they could find the key to the code, it would tell them one hell of a lot. Clint had a case where a man who developed code-breakers for comps was murdered. He had left a program. Clint was trying it out. If he could find any base at all ... the numbers were all less than four hundred. What could that mean? A page and line number in a book? There was one number, then a hyphen, then another number, then a hyphen, then a number between one and eight.

It was logical that was a page, line and word number.

Too many sentences had more than eight words. It was something else.

Whatever, it was useless, if he didn't know the book. What book was mentioned in all this by any of them?

Clint grinned. Dr. Freud would make a case of her. Freudian slip?

He Googled "Freud" to find what books he wrote. He then checked the page numbers in the books.

Nothing – except the references to something called "A Student's Guide to Dr. Sigmund Freud" in a College Reference Library edition. Expensive. 487 pages.

He thought for a moment. That would be a book almost no university in Central America would have. It was for medical students. Advanced medical students.

Granada? They would have most things. They were

closest.

Stupid. Gault would have a copy. He would even have it here, if he came to get those sheets.

Clint grinned. Even better! Gault was supposedly in the hospital in David. If Mittermann was in on some kind of scheme with him, he would have to appear to really be there the way Clint had pretended to be in Bocas Town.

Clint called Mittermann and said he had to ask Gault a few questions about Maria. He was owed answers to those questions. Seeing he was in the hospital Clint could be there in the morning to ask the questions, then could tell the Campbells whether or not what they suspected was true. It would be a way to make very damned sure Maria didn't bother any of them again.

Mittermann mumbled around for a couple of minutes, then said Gault might not be in the hospital, anymore. Clint said he could talk with him anywhere. He would have to stay in a hotel there for three days to be sure there was no infection. If he didn't want to do that, the police wouldn't allow him to leave until they investigated how and why he was shot. He told them it was an accident. It would be normal for him to stay until the doctors released him.

"It would be normal if he was already scheduled to go and did," Mittermann argued.

"No. It would look like he was running from someone," Clint replied. "He'd be a fool to do anything to make them suspicious."

"He's staying at the City of David. I suppose he'll be here for part of tomorrow, anyhow."

Clint told him, "Thanks. It probably doesn't have anything to do with his case. It was about something that was said about him at a party in Jamaica."

That seemed to relieve Mittermann.

Clint caught the plane to David. He was there, just at dark. He would be expected to meet Gault in the morning. Gault wouldn't be there tonight until late. He had a date.

Clint had a good meal in the restaurant at the hotel. He talked with the man at the desk about his friend from Haiti. He said he was supposed to meet him tomorrow, but came in early. Would he ring his room, please?

The clerk rang 306. There was no answer. He said Mr. Gault was, apparently, not there. Clint thanked him again and went back into the restaurant. A few minutes later, he went back through the lobby, toward the door. He slipped into the open elevator when no one was looking.

It was easy enough to get into the room. Clint has experience in that. He knew how to read the card and to use the hotel entry code. The computer was on the desk, with the charger on it. Clint took a memory stick from his pocket, went to the inicio page, to documents, and to a folder labeled "Books," to find "Freud" listed. He copied the book to the memory stick, cleared the screen, put the comp back on charge, and left. In the morning, he met with Gault and asked why people kept saying at that party that he was a drug supplier to France and England – did he know that was being said?

He was actually shocked! *No* one ever said he had anything to do with the drug trade. Who was saying it?

"Cori heard it. She said that must be why you're here, but it couldn't be – because it was just something she heard. She wasn't sure who said it, except he was an obnoxious sort of pig who kept pawing at her.

"I don't think much of you, but I know how that kind of thing can fuck up your reputation among those political asses. If you didn't know it, you probably aren't messed up in that crap. If you knew it, there might be a basis. You might be after her. As it is, she's done you a favor."

"She did that! I can drop a little word and that shithead – I can guess who it was – won't say another word about me again. Ever. I will say to you that my reputation is that I give one warning, then act. Never two. Never say a thing, unless you are prepared to follow your words with action. One or two times, a long time ago, and the problem doesn't arise again."

Clint said that was all he wanted to know. Thanks.

"You came here only to ask that?"

"The answer was in the way you reacted, not in the words you used. You were actually shocked. It was all over your face. I can believe that. I couldn't ever be sure from a phone call. People in certain situations are prone to prevaricate."

"I think you scare me. I hope there is never reason you will be after me."

Clint grinned. He said he had a reputation to uphold, himself.

He left.

Clint stretched, sighed, turned on his computer, and stuck the memory stick in the USB port to bring up the book.

It was in German.

So what? He could use the code to write what came up and have a friend translate.

Assuming that the first number was the page number, the second the line number and the third was ...?

He cut and pasted all he had, putting the whole line on the page. Most of it was the same on both sets of sheets. Only the lists noted were very much different.

Clint studied the thing awhile. He didn't know enough, but one thing caught his eye in the main paragraphs. The one through eight seemed to be the number of words included, starting from a period. Thus seven came out to be "This later was seen to be the major" and the next line had a one that said "Directions" followed by the line with a four. "To take this further" followed by something he couldn't translate from his meager knowledge of German. It did tell him, he hoped, how the code was read. Four and a half hours later, he had the whole thing, except the lists. There had to be a different base to that code. It was the same three number system, but none was ended with a number higher than three. The first number was no higher than four. The second number was as high as fifty five.

Clint couldn't find a key to that.

He called Judi, who came over to look at the lists. She went from the first page of the book to the end. The end had appendices and reference to footnotes and credits. Four pages.

She took the first one, 2-37-2. She went to page 2, to credit 37, and to the second name. Marks, Konrad. The next was 1-19-3. That was strange. The first name on the credits there was Reighter, Adolf Enrique. There was no third name.

"Ah!" Clint said. "The third word is Enrique. Marks and Enrique. Mean anything?"

"Cori said there was some German attaché named Marks at that party."

"And an Enrique somebody. I think this is a very important list. We have to get a translator we can trust."

"Ben. He speaks German. I've heard him."

Ben was a close friend and neighbor. He was involved in a couple of cases. Clint knew he could trust him. Judi called and asked him to come over. He said half an hour. He had to get his latest boyfriend to the water taxi. He was on the way, right now.

Oh, yeah. He was gay.

Clint and Judi translated the rest of the list of names. Twelve. There were four names that were different on the two lists.

The list from Gault had him and someone named Fred Sanders, a woman named Gisela Christianson, and a man named Yohn Kopec changed on Maria's list. Gault was changed to Markos Jardín, Gisela Bendetti was changed to Oscar, Sanders was changed to Velasquez and Kopec was changed to Linderman.

When Ben showed up, Judi explained what they'd done. She told him about the lists.

"It would seem, unless there's another Oscar in this, that friend Mittermann plans to become a leader in this stupid scheme," Clint said.

"Who's Oscar?" Ben asked.

"You don't want to know," Judi said.

"A CIA asshole," Clint said. "I think maybe we can bring this particular pot to a pretty fast boil."

Clint's cell phone buzzed. He looked at the caller ID and answered, to hear Luis say, "It seems the lovely Maria has decided to stay with Cecilio for a few days. She is in fear of someone, by what we can understand of her very poor Spanish, or she is someone to be feared, because of a bruja in some other place, or something. We have placed her into a room that can be locked to be sure no one can get to her. She has spoken to only Cecilio. She knows I speak Spanish, thus we let her know not that I am even here."

"Thanks, Luis. If Cecilio could get a message to her with his own poor Spanish that someone named Oscar and someone named Gault are looking for her and he feels that they are dangerous people she should be protected from...?"

"I think, perhaps, I can manage that."

They chatted a minute more. It seemed Maria was trying to get through to them that she was working for a powerful witch who would turn them all into zombies, or something. They were acting like they thought she was saying a witch was looking for her to turn her into a zombie. It was great fun. They kept assuring her that no witch could get to her. The comarca had a witch of their own to give her an amulet of garlic to keep zombies and vampires away.

"What was that about?" Judi asked, when he rang off.

"Maria is being held in protective custody on the comarca because, from what Cecilio can understand of her very poor Spanish, some witch is looking for her to turn her into a zombie. Maybe him into a zombie. Maybe both. She didn't make any sense. He locked her in where no one can get to her and will have the bruja make a spell against zombies."

"Her poor Spanish? Hell, she speaks perfect Spanish!" Judi grinned. "He must only speak dialect. Naturally, he can't understand Spanish, beyond buenos dias."

"Well, I was trying to understand his dialect, and may have it wrong," Clint said, in excellent dialect. "I think this is a great break! I'll call friend Gault and tell him we found a list in the kitchen at Obilio's place that's in German. I can give him the list of names that are the same in any language. Oscar is on it. He isn't."

"That could piss him off!" Judi said. Ben laughed, and said maybe Gault would want to turn Oscar into a zombie. This could be a great horror movie. *Zombies In the Mist* or *Terror In the Timbers.*

"Maybe *Zombies In the Timbers* or *Terrors In the Mist*," Judi suggested.

"It would make a good Keystone Kop show, with this bunch of clowns," Clint suggested. "Maybe *Charlie Chaplin Meets the Chumps,* or something."

He called Gault. He said (with his innocent act) that they had found the list and translated the names. He said, seeing what had happened, that Oscar might be Mittermann, which would explain his even knowing about it. Don't trust him.

He could hear the rage in Gault's voice, though he was trying to sound like it was nice to know, and thanks. Clint hung up, and said, "I think the thing that's boiling is Gault's temper. This could get interesting."

"It could be deadly," Judi warned.

"Yeah, but not for us," Clint agreed. "I think, the only way to stop it is to just let them kill each other off. Just so no more innocent bystanders are drawn in, that's fine with me."

They waited for a couple of hours, but didn't hear

anything more. Ben had translated the sheets that were made by Claire Auber. The original list was the original group. The second was how the group would become as soon as they got those four out of it. The main paragraphs, except for that item on the second set, was mostly laying out who was in charge (Auber) and who was to handle which part. Most of that was supplying funds and personnel when the thing was set in motion. The weak part was having no control of who, outside of the group, became involved. It was important that whoever else could be terrorized into silence, if they learned too much. She could handle that. She was the most feared witch in Haiti. Everyone in the Latin American countries could be threatened with untold horrors, if they crossed her.

It might not be too easy to set it in motion, now. It seemed some of the major players weren't too happy about the arrangements.

The main thing they learned was from adding up what happened there with the Campbells and Maria and Pablo. The way Clint figured, Mittermann was in Panamá. He had discovered the plot, and cut himself in. He wouldn't be someone Auber could terrorize with her mighty witch act. It would be up to him to get Gault involved to where he could be knocked over.

Maria latched onto the Campbells as an excuse to come to Panamá. Gault was conned into coming when he was told that Maria had a list of the group that was about to fall into the hands of the CIA. It was the use of terror and threats of witches and zombies and so forth that would scare the Panamanians into not acting against them. The list was to be given to Mittermann when Gault, et al, were handled. It was his contract.

Well, maybe some Panamanians would be terrorized

by some witch in Haiti, particularly the blacks. Not the Indios. That was a huge mistake. You can't terrorize the Indios here. They're a very practical people. It went wrong because Clint Faraday got involved. They didn't know who did that. Someone told a friend of Faraday's that the Campbells were not what they seemed as a way to get suspicions started against them. Then they met Judi Lum. It went straight to hell from that point, because she told Faraday what the Campbells were really like. Just normal people.

If they had simply shot Gault and the other three in the head, it would have probably worked. As it turned out, the complications drug the scheme down. Nothing worked out the way the brilliant Claire planned. She didn't take into consideration that Faraday and the Indios would find her to be a joke. Most Panamanians aren't superstitious. Their witches are more medicine women than witches, in the traditional sense. They don't claim extraordinary powers.

Maybe that was way off on a tangent, but it made a kind of sense. Nothing else did. Claire Auber was an egomaniac who thought she was smarter than everyone around her, because the witches were feared in Haiti and Jamaica. It was a fantasy in her own mind. Most of the others either feared witches or knew she could wield a lot of power – on those islands.

Which came down to Mittermann discovering a silly plot and using it to his own advantage. These people were wealthy enough to where he could get a few millions, personally, before the scheme collapsed. He figured wrong, too. Claire Auber thought she was a terror, but she was a joke. It would almost be funny, if innocent people hadn't been drawn into it. Doom was definitely involved. The plot was doomed from the get-go.

Clint thought about it awhile, then decided to wait for a couple of days to see what developed. He called Cecilio and said to tell Maria it was all a misunderstanding. Let her go late this afternoon. Her own people would handle things, from that point. Gault called him in the wee hours and said that some gringo by the name of Mittermann had left David and gone toward the home of some Indio named Obilio in the mountains. He understood Obilio was in Bocas Town with his wife, so what was he up to?

"He doesn't know I found the lists, does he?"

"Not from me."

"Then he has some way that Maria told him where she left it. He's going after it."

"That could be a mistake."

"Uh-huh. Talk to you tomorrow when they find one or the other of their bodies."

"Sounds like a plan."

Judi called from her deck for Clint to answer his phone. Gault was trying to get in touch. He seemed very anxious about something. He hadn't struck her as the anxious type.

Clint turned the thing off when he didn't want to be bothered all night with those people. He went in and turned it on. It rang about three minutes later.

"Faraday? Gault here. I've been trying to reach you for hours."

"I turned the phone off for the night. It's the only way to get any sleep, lately. What can I do for you?"

"I need to know if Maria's free somewhere around here. She's the only one I care about, so far as danger to myself is concerned. She is one cold bitch! I doubt she ever feels anything, at all."

"She was at Cecilio's until yesterday afternoon. He let her go. It seemed he thought she was hiding from a witch in Haiti or something. He locked her into a shed where he could protect her. His Spanish sucks. He told her the witch woman said she would put a spell on her that would keep zombies away. She kept blabbing on about him or her being turned into zombies if he or she didn't do something. He couldn't understand her, so protected her from zombies."

"Zombies?" Gault giggled. He said Mittermann doesn't answer his phone since midnight or a little after when he tried to call him. He might have met the lovely Maria, unexpectedly. Clint said anything was possible. Maybe he met the zombie, instead.

After Gault rang off, Clint called Luis and said to *carefully* go to see what, if anything, was going on at

Obilio's place. Luis said he would go in a few minutes. It seemed quiet, but he had seen Pablo. He would be careful to an extreme.

Judi came in. Clint suggested they could go to breakfast at Don Chicho's. She agreed, and they strolled into town. Mike Campbell was in Don Chicho's with a local girl. They said "hello"s and such. Mike was going to the hotel. The family were going to head for San Andreas. Matt was talking about going back to Chitre and Las Tablas to look for a place. He wanted to stay in Panamá. Mike agreed, but Cori and Mark wanted to go back to the states.

Everybody could go where they wanted. They were an independent lot. Mike might stay here or go to David, instead of San Andreas. He wanted to go to Rio Sereno and Puerto Armuelles, like Clint had suggested.

Clint and Judi walked down to the ferry dock and back, just for the exercise. They spoke with a number of people they knew, plus a couple of tourists who wanted to know the best restaurants and such. They decided to go to Red Frog by boat, then to go out in the Caribbean to see if the tuna were in and biting. That would take most of the day and would let them relax. They could use some relaxation.

They were out in the Caribbean, catching a lot of sun and not too much else, when Clint's phone buzzed. It was Luis. He sounded excited.

"I hope that animal doesn't ever decide to come after me!" Luis greeted.

"Which animal is that?"

"That Maria woman. You think Pablo was torn up? You should see Mittermann! At least Pablo died fast. Mittermann didn't."

"She thinks he found her lists ... no, that was what she

was there for. To get rid of Gault and give him the new list. His list was his contract. I guess she just didn't like him."

"She tortured him like that because she didn't like him?"

"She's not a very nice lady." Clint could picture Luis giving the phone the bird. They talked a bit longer. Luis said the police chopper was coming in. He took it on himself to call them to the comarca, seeing it was some gringo who was dead.

Clint told Judi about it. She shuddered. It could have been her and Ann when they had them at that cave. On their way back to Clint's house, they got another call from Luis. Maria was seen getting on a bus to David on the other side of the mountain, ten minutes ago. She would probably take the Calderas bus to the highway, then get the Boquete bus at the junction.

Clint decided not to call Gault to warn him. He could fend for himself with his special bunch.

They cleaned up and went to the Nine Degrees for an expensive, but very good, dinner with Ben and a man he met at the surf shop by the Hotel Bocas del Toro. John Guest. Judi said she was jealous. She admired his taste in men.

They joked and had a good time for awhile. Judi went to El Refugio with a man she was dating on and off. Clint went to The Rip Tide, Ben went to The Iguana with his friend. Clint talked with several people there, then went home for a decent night's rest. When he was passing the Mondo Taitu, he saw a girl he had met the year before. She decided she would go home with him. Last year was so good she kept comparing him with other men. They almost always came up short. She wanted to see if he still had it.

The night wasn't restful, to any degree, but it was a great night, all the same!

In the morning, he had an e-mail saying that Dave would be back that afternoon. There were six or eight ads he erased.

He would go to Chiriqui Grande, today. He had some unfinished business there. He could go on to Cusapín to visit friends there for a day or two, or return to Bocas Town. He would wait until he was there to decide.

He got a call while he was in Chiriqui Grande from Sam, the police jefe in David. It seemed that a woman's body was found close to Anastasia, by the river. She had his name and phone number on a piece of paper in her pocket, but no other identification.

"What did she look like?" Clint asked.

"Latina, with some white and some negro, pretty, but not beautiful, about twenty three or thirty three. Hard to tell. The autopsy would get it. Maybe her prints. She didn't seem to be local.

"It's probably Maria Garza," Clint said. "Pull her passport and check the prints to that."

Sam said he'd try. It might work. He could pull the passport photo off the net.

He called back ten minutes later to say it was Maria.

"How did she die?" Clint asked.

"We can't find anything. She seems to have gone down by the river, laid down, and died."

Clint was thoughtful, then smirked to himself. Maybe Auber wanted her out of the way, too. He wondered if maybe Gault hadn't brought along some kind of voodoo poison from Haiti. Maybe it was someone he didn't even know about. He wouldn't worry about it.

He did sort of wonder if Gault was still around. It was altogether possible he was dead of some strange poison, or something. That would fit the rest of this. If he was, Auber was getting rid of all the people and evidence against her. That would mean that whoever was doing the dirty work for her was a total fool. He or she would then be the only evidence around against her. He or she was handling the way people who knew too much were disposed of.

Clint wondered about that piece of paper. Why did Maria have that? Did she plan to come after him? Why? Would he ever know enough about this for it to begin to make sense? He didn't believe for one second that he had all the answers. He might not even have a large percent of them.

He would worry about it some other time. She couldn't come after him, now, that was sure.

He headed back to Bocas Town. He wasn't in the mood for Cusapín, today.

Back in Bocas Town, Clint went to several places to listen to the gossip. Douglas was sitting with Jim at the Golden Grill. He sat to see if anything was new, but it was more of the same. Tom came to join them and Clint left. Try as he might, he simply couldn't like the ass.

He went to the China to stock up on groceries, then home with them. He got a call from Gault. It was from Haiti. He wanted to know if Clint knew what was happening to the group on the lists.

"They're getting knocked off. How many of the eighteen of you are still alive?·"

"Eighteen? So you also found the list I buried. I thought you had.

"There are eleven of us left. I think."

"Did you get Maria, or was it someone else?"

"She's dead? Someone else."

"Claire seems to be getting rid of possible witnesses

against her.”

“Someone will have to get rid of her. Her voodoo can’t protect her when some of us know it’s mostly crap. She’s very good with poisons.”

“Yeah. She’s a homicidal maniac, as far as I’m concerned.”

“Good description! I have to see if I can stay alive, or if it will be her. It can’t be both. She’s a sociopathic homicidal maniac would be a small bit more accurate, I believe.

“I like you, Clint. You aren’t scared of any of us. You shoot as straight as we’ll allow. Thanks.” He hung up.

Clint sort of wondered if he would survive. As he said, both of them couldn’t.

Clint sort of liked him, too. He had a charm.

Obilio came to say he and Lila were going home on the late bus. They would get to David late, would stay at a friend’s place, then go up to the house tomorrow.

“Be very careful what you eat and drink there,” Clint warned. “Remember that Maria left that sleep potion for Ann. She might have left some other nasty little surprises around.”

“Doesn’t need saying.”

This was probably over, for their part. It had been a little terrifying and a little fun and a little a lot of other things. Clint still didn’t have a clue as to what was really going on. He probably never would.

He never would if Auber survived. Gault would call to let him know he won. He would want to gloat.

C’est la vie!

He and Judi went to The Lemon Grass for dinner. Dave came in to play a few numbers. He asked if anything came of the message he left about the Campbell people.

"Oh, it was sorta interesting. They were alright. Not boring," Clint answered.

C. D. Moulton's works are available on most major outlets as printed or e-books. CD writes the CD Grimes, PI, mysteries, the Det. Lt. Nick Storie mysteries, the Clint Faraday mysteries, the Flight of the Maita science fiction series, books on orchid culture and many others of many types. Mystery, adventure, intrigue, science fiction, humor, fantasy, paranormal, mild erotica, and factual.

www.ingramcontent.com/pod-product-compliance
Lightning Source LLC
Chambersburg PA
CBHW060218170726
48004CB00014B/604